Witches

Witches

Georgia L. Jones

SEVENTH STAR PRESS

Cover art: Aaron Drown Design

Editor: Scott Sandridge

Published by Seventh Star Press, LLC.

ISBN Number: 978-1-941706-51-0

Seventh Star Press

www.seventhstarpress.com

info@seventhstarpress.com

Publisher's Note:

Witches is a work of fiction. All names, characters, and places are the product of the author's imagination, used in fictitious manner. Any resemblances to actual persons, places, locales, events, etc. are purely coincidental.

Printed in the United States of America

Second Edition

INTRODUCTION

As my eyes opened I realized the vision was upon me. It grabbed my soul and pushed me into an alert state. I had experienced pieces of the same vision all winter and every evening when I woke from my rest. The vision was thick in my mind, telling me the time would soon come to leave my sanctuary again. The earthy smell here called to me.

I thought of my death from the human world and how I plummeted into this world. I thought of the time I had lost on Vicus last fall and was saddened briefly when I thought of the nine years I had lost there. For me it seemed like only last year, but it was 2020 now. It had been almost ten years since my death.

I couldn't help but think of the human family I had left behind. It had not been by choice, but the pain that had accompanied the transition had made me even stronger, and the warrior inside me was strong.

Samantha Garrett had long since become just a memory, and I, Samoda, was a warrior who had been entrusted to rid this world of the evil that doesn't belong here. I would lead my brethren Warriors into battles for all of eternity, or until my ultimate annihilation, whichever came first.

I knew I would be chosen to become an Elder by Nuem. I knew at some point he would make it official. I had no way of knowing when, just that it would happen. I could feel the Elder Spirit surging through me. Tarvoti, the only remaining Elder, was no longer a maternal figure in my non-beating heart. She was an equal.

As I thought of my beloved, Drake, I found happiness and a smile graced my lips. The love that we shared was completely unconditional. There were no bounds. There was no need for boundaries. Our actual souls were entwined as one. He was part of me and I part of him.

Every evening, when we woke from our rest, Drake and Tarvoti listened intently as I gave them details of the visions I had. They believed in my visions maybe more than I did. As far as we knew I was the only Warrior who dreamed. Those dreams were visions of the future. Sometimes they came in glimpses and sometimes they came in orderly detailed scenes. I was being dragged through the future with each one. Although it felt like a curse most of the time, it was really a gift from the God that I chose to serve, Nuem.

One thing was for certain in all of our minds, there was another battle brewing. The Avorians had taken hold in the rural United States. We would be attacked again, and this time their plan was more organized and much more deceitful than the last. Instead of infiltrating the Warrior community they had gone straight for the humans. The Avorian Army was building itself strong, because they knew we would come. This time they were going to be ready. They were pulling the humans deeper into their plot and forcing our hand.

The human girl with two faces would either be the human savior or their annihilation. I knew this. I also knew she would give us much grief. She would put William's soul in danger and possibly lead to our demise as well. Kali Rose Marriot could be the end of the human race as we know it. She could single- handedly be the one that brings ruin and ash to the cities of the world.

With the looming threat hanging above us, we were anxiously awaiting the time of battle. As always, we were not scared of our fate, we embraced it, and were ready to seek it out. It was innate to our species. We were the Warriors for Nuem, our God who resides on Atheria, and we stood for good against evil of all kinds. Self-preservation was merely an afterthought for us.

Our duty was simply to keep the balance, not destroy it. As I had already learned there are demons of this world that belong here. Without bad there could be no good. So the balance was all- important. When the Avorians enact a plan to take over or completely eradicate the humans, we step in.

Long ago, before humans were created, Nuem and Avore lived here on earth. There were, of course, battles between the two and all of their creatures that inhabited this place. They became bored with one another and created humans for their entertainment. However, the agreement was that no creatures, good or bad, could ever mate with the humans. Of course, we Atherians have always stuck to that pact, but the Avorians did not. Evil was quickly bred into the humans, some more than others.

Our laws here on earth are few. We can live as we choose as long as we entertain our duty to aid Nuem when needed, and as my senses woke and the warrior came to life inside me, I knew it was time. Today Drake, Tarvoti, and I would be swept up by Woden, the spirit of the element of the skies, and be taken back to the United States. We would meet up with our old friend William and would begin our journey to the center of the country where evil had taken its root.

We left the cave and ran into the woods. We raced through the trees until the ocean beat against the coast. We had spotted Woden's spiraling turbulence from the treetops and one by one we jumped into his grasp as he spun us into another realm and dropped us in the middle of New York City. We all knew where we were going and under cover of night we ran through the city to William's home…

CHAPTER ONE

GOING HOME

T *he storm last fall brought with it a plague of wild animals. I guess they ended up here to seek shelter in the thick Ozarks woods. Nobody seemed to be able to get a good look at them. There were lots of death notices lately, and people were a little more scared to go out at night. There were rumors, of course, always rumors, of shadows that go bump in the night. Most rational people chalked it up to rabid animals. It rained for so long and so hard that maybe some of them just went crazy looking for shelter and food.*

The coroner, Mr. Cobb wasn't for certain what had gotten a hold of Grandma. As he tried to offer me his condolences, he put his arm around me and said, "Had to of been big, whatever it was, she was tough as boot leather and a perfect shot with the ole shotgun." I knew he was right. If it could kill her, it could have killed anyone.

"Thank ya, Mr. Cobb." I said politely. "I better get over to Mr. Button's office. He's got some paperwork for me."

"Will your sister, Seline, be joining ya out there, or are ya going it alone, Kali?" He asked solemnly.

"I don't think she will make it. She's pretty busy ya know." I knew she really was busy, but I didn't find that to be an excuse. The truth of the matter was when she left, she never looked back. She hadn't been home since.

It was a short drive down the street to Mr. Button's office. I could have walked the block, but it was hot and I was tired. I pulled in and looked up at the office. I remembered as a child walking freely through town with not a care in the world. Now, here I was readying myself for the finalities of Grandma's estate. I wanted to cry, but held back the tears for a later time. I kept my mind busy thinking of the grass between each crack in the old sidewalk as I walked up it.

Mr. Button's office smelled like an old dentist office. His secretary pointed me to have a seat, without a word, and disappeared to let him know that I was there.

"Kali Rose Marriot, it's good to see you dear." He said as he came through the door and grabbed me in a big hug. "I'm so sorry to hear about your Grandma. Come on back. We'll get this done quick for you."

"Thank you Mr. Button." I said as I followed him through the heavy door into his office.

It didn't take long for the paperwork. He had it all in order, and we didn't have many decisions to make. Grandma already had everything taken care of. I couldn't help but be thankful for that.

"Dewey, over at Mount Point Cemetery, called me..." he frowned sadly, "...he said the service would be on Friday. I'll be there."

"I really do thank you Mr. Button." I said with a forced smile as I stood to leave.

"You know, Kali, I known your folks a long time." He reached up to scratch his balding head as he paused. "If you need anything, you know where I'm at. Don't think twice about calling me."

I wished for a moment that Seline was here. As twins, I wondered sometimes if she could feel when I really missed her and just ignored it or if she didn't feel anything at all. I knew that she was still bitter about our back-woodsy, poverty-stricken childhood, but I still felt that it was selfish of her not to at least show up. I also knew that she was different. She really was selfish and mean spirited, she always had been. Most people that met her didn't like her or, at the very least, didn't care to be around her.

As I walked out of the lawyer's office I felt tears welling in my eyes. I already missed her. My grandmother had raised us for part of our childhood. Her and my Grandpa took us when my Mom was having a rough time. Mom would come and go frequently, but our main care was left to our grandparents. Seline and I were only twelve when Mom died. She was buried up at Mount Point next to where Grandma would be laid to rest.

I could still hear Grandma calling to us to come in after we were done playing for the night. "Kali, Seline, time ta come in, fore the wolves carry ya off," she would holler at the top of her lungs. We always listened. Grandma really wasn't mean. She was just kind of scary. We never sought to intentionally piss her off.

When Grandpa fell sick, he died shortly afterwards. The drinking and the cigars had gotten him. Later, I was certain he probably had cancer in his liver and his lungs, but at the time, Grandma just told us that it had finally got him. She told us there were demons in those types of indulgences and that the demons would take our souls to hell if we took part in either or both, and maybe that's why she spent days after the funeral keeping the fire out back burning, occasionally adding different herbs from the yard and chanting things that were of no use to a child. Maybe, just maybe, she was trying to save his soul from the demons that had gotten him. Of course we patronized her and said we believed her. Grandma would never lie to us. She was just trying to keep us innocent as long as she could.

Now all that was left of her was the deed to the old homestead that was solely mine. It was tucked away in the cloth that I had remembered seeing inside a drawer in her old writing desk. The burlap was old and worn. It was probably stitched right from an old sack of potatoes many years ago.

I thought of how hot the day was as I stepped onto the

sidewalk to return to my car. I had already driven two hours this morning to get here and was feeling tired from the grief and the heat. I would spend the next few days at the homestead and then head back home. I hadn't decided what I would do with it yet and was too exhausted to think about it right now.

As I walked, I noticed the car that had parked next to mine. It was fancier than any I had ever seen before, and my first thought was that someone in town must have won the lottery. Then I noticed the people walking towards it. They had come out of the café next door. I didn't even vaguely recognize them. There were two men and two women, and they were magnificent. The women were exact opposites: one had long wavy blonde hair and other ones' was black and silky. The men were extraordinarily handsome. They were both very tall and looked as though they worked out every single day. I allowed myself the pleasure of gazing at them, after all it wasn't often that I was afforded such a sight here, or anywhere for that matter. They all had a rather serious gait and seemed as though they were on a mission.

The blonde woman's expression softened a little as she turned and looked back at me. Her eyes were the most amazing blue I had ever seen. It was as though the ocean and clouds had been mixed to concoct a blue cocktail that was nearly indescribable. The smile that she shot my direction was reassuring and comforting as well as slightly scary. There was something in that smile, something that gave me goose bumps. Maybe it was just the fact that I hadn't ever encountered anyone like this ever before. Most people with the power that this group seemed to possess didn't bother smiling at regular people like me, which incited a slight blush on my part.

As they got into their car, the dark-haired woman's eyes caught mine. They were hypnotic. I felt comfortable in them, and they seemed familiar and kind. With a single blink I felt the blood drain from my head. As it began to swim, I felt flushed and hot. They pulled away before I got to my car door.

In Southern Missouri, July 8th could be as daunting as any

day in the summer. Sweat beaded on my forehead just as I opened the car door. I felt sweet relief from the heat as I turned on the air and drove away, but the gnawing pain of the grief was stuck inside me. From that I could find no solace.

It was a sleepy day in the small town. It only took a minute to get through the main part of town, which consisted of one street full of hometown businesses. There was a small grocery store, a post office, the bank, a corner café, the local watering hole, of course the lawyer's office, and a few other Mom and Pop stores littering the street. That was the sum of it.

I remembered it well. On occasion my sister and I would come to town with Grandpa on Saturday to get some groceries and other supplies. He would usually visit the Lana Lace Tavern for an hour or so to have a drink, and we were left unattended with a few dollars to roam around and stay out of trouble.

As I passed the school, I couldn't help but remember back to that era in my life. We started here in third grade and went through the tenth. One building housed the entire educational facility, including the superintendent's office.

As I thought back, I drove the wedge of sadness a little further into my heart, remembering my freshman year. We were up to fourteen in our grade with the new girl, Heather. Then in October that year, Nick Cater died. He and I knew each other well and he was the first boy that I ever kissed. Our class dwindled back to the thirteen that it had been since we had started years before. At least until the next year when Grandma saw no need for a formal education, so on our sixteenth birthday we quit.

She saw the public school system as a waste of time. There was nothing they could teach us that we really needed in life. Every time the subject came up she would get kind of huffy and say, "It's jus' a waste. Ya need to be learnin' how ta cook and sew. There ain't nothin' ya need to learn that we can't teach ya, right here."

Later in life, when we decided we needed it, we had both gotten our GEDs. Seline went on to college to study psychology, and I just chose to open my own business.

She would be considered much more successful than I by most social standards. She opened her own practice after she got her doctorate degree. I just opened up the "Hippie Shop." I sold everything from handmade bead necklaces to tea leaves for reading. It was a decent living, and it was honest. I didn't have to pretend to be something I was not.

I turned onto the state highway heading out of town. The rural highway was lined with huge farms. Some of them had large silos and hundreds or even thousands of head of cattle. There was a pig farm on the left side of the road. As I passed it I knew I was getting close to the old farm. It was just far enough past it that you could only smell it when the wind was blowing just right. On normal days you couldn't.

When I turned up the drive I felt like I should see her coming around the corner to see who was there. Instead, the door was fastened shut and nobody was around.

I didn't ever remember visiting, after I was grown, and ever finding her inside. She was definitely the outdoors type.

The old house was more dilapidated than I had remembered. After Grandpa had passed it got worse and worse. She would use makeshift repairs to fix the larger holes to keep the weather out and the old stove was always stoked, even in the summer, for cooking. She had refused to let me buy her a more modern one. I often wondered why she wouldn't fix it up or just move into town to the assisted living center. She would have none of that, though. Grandma had enjoyed her living circumstances. She would not have been happy anywhere else. She wouldn't even use the more modern amenities such as electricity most of the time.

She had lived here since she was born. I had heard the stories of how, with her mom and dad and thirteen brothers and sisters, they had managed here in the old house. They slept stacked nearly on top of one another in the winter to try and stay warm.

It certainly wasn't for lack of space. In its day this house would have been the glory of the area. It stood with twelve foot ceilings on the bottom floor and ten foot on the second floor. It had five bedrooms upstairs. I would guess it was about three thousand square feet in area. Yet, now it stood there like a creaky old mansion. The yard was grown up in spots giving the old house a look of abandonment and violation. I couldn't find fear inside me as I shut the car off and opened the door.

When I got out of my car, I felt a lump building in my throat. It would be the first time I was ever here without her. She would have hovered and warned me to get out of this or that, or tell me to go pick this or that out of the yard and add it to the soup or something.

It would be strange going through her things. I thought of that as I pushed the door open. The latch on the outside was kind of a rope rigging lock. No need for a key. On the inside a long piece of wood leaned against the wall to be laid across the whole frame to keep it closed and locked from any intruders that might make their way out here in no man's land.

I flipped the switch beside the door and began to survey the task that lay before me. One out of the six bulbs that hung from the old chandelier in the center of the hallway came on, I felt lucky that one worked. The dust that clung to my finger from the light switch made me smile. It hadn't been touched for years most likely. I let out a heavy sigh and thought since it was going to be up to me, I may as well suck it up and get to it.

I made my way through the old hallway, the kitchen, and into the pantry that lay at the back of the house where I opened up the back door to let some more air filter through. Even with the draft of the front and back door opened it was stifling inside. I could see why she spent so much time outside. On a cool fall day it may have been okay, but here, today, the air was so still I could hardly find my own breath.

I had come to the realization that I had nothing better to do right now. The kids were all grown, and I had a lot of free time on my hands lately. My marriage had failed when the kids moved out, and I had closed up the shop till this was taken care of. I would spend as long as it took to take care of everything here that I needed to. I knew that realistically it would take more than a few days. This house was filled with several generations of things, and it would not be easy to sort through.

I had called Tabby and Trent, my children, to let them know. They had never been close to Grandma, and as I figured, they weren't going to be able to make it. All thirteen of her brothers and sisters had perished before her and none of them had ever had children so I had no cousins to get a hold of. I guessed that I would be the only family member in attendance on Friday, although I was certain that several friends would show up.

I turned to look in the back door, and with a pained heart made a plan to achieve my task. I knew that Grandma's bedroom would be the most difficult, so I thought I would start in the kitchen. I would get through the downstairs, then head up.

I went from room to room, first opening the old interior wooden shutters on the windows, then the windows that still retained screens on them. I had at least one window in each room open when the clouds started to roll in. The slight breeze that wafted through felt good.

I made trips back and forth to the car unloading everything quickly, trying to beat the storm that seemed to be looming on the horizon. At least I had thought enough ahead to buy boxes, packing tape and trash bags. I spread it all out in the living room for easy access and began folding and taping the bottom of the boxes.

I started in the kitchen. As I cleaned, I was sure that Grandma hadn't actually thrown anything away in years that could be recycled into something, anything, else. I smiled as I thought of her being the epitome of 'going green.' I sorted through plastic and aluminum and put them in their proper bags. I would take them to town tomorrow to drop in the recycling bins behind the store.

I had pretty much gotten the kitchen sorted through and went to the pantry to start on it. The rows were neatly lined with the canned tuna in one line, corn in another, and so forth and so on.

I got down on my knees to look at the bottom row. There were jugs of homemade wine. I started pulling them out, and at the very back of the shelf I found some papers. Scrawled across the tops were names, Elderberry, Strawberry, Apple, and Potato. I didn't look at the rest, but tucked them away in a smaller box to read later. I knew they were her homemade wine recipes. Grandma had always enjoyed her wine, and the only kind she would ever drink was what she had made herself.

I cleaned as I went, using the rainwater that she had always kept in barrels outside the house. They were still full from the recent rains we had. I thought of her intently each time I threw the old dirty water out and refreshed it with the clean. I know it is what she would have wanted. I could almost feel her smiling down on me as I thought of it. She always saved the tap water for drinking and would say 'never know when the well might run dry.'

She was a quirky old lady, and one that I loved dearly. I nearly began to cry as I cleaned and let my mind wander to a time when she would have been here to direct me in my tasks. I scrubbed the surfaces feverishly, not wanting to miss a spot.

I began shuffling around the jars of spices and herbs that were stowed away in their old hand-marked containers on the top shelf. There were different names, some that I didn't recognize and some that I did, like Angelica, which she rubbed on our chest when we were sick and of course made tea for us to drink. Grandma had grown all of them in different spots throughout the back yard. I was certain I would never be able to keep them all straight in my mind and that would certainly be a gift lost to a dead generation.

I had to get a chair to reach the very back. As I pulled the herbs off the shelves, wiped the bottles and put them on a lower shelf that would be easier to pack, I noticed a small door in the back corner. I stood on my tip toes to reach it. The small knob was brittle, and as I tugged on it a small sliver of it broke off. I looked around and spotted a butter knife on the counter across the room. I grabbed it and pried the door open.

The cubbyhole wasn't very deep and its complete contents consisted of an old dirty leather-bound book and two smaller ones. The smaller volumes had covers made of starched burlap. I thumbed quickly through the books, and all of them had notes scribbled throughout them. I sat them on top of the papers in the box. I would make a point to dig through the box later and read everything.

I looked at the old Big Ben windup clock on the mantle as it struck six and decided it was time to take a break. The day had been exhausting. I had gotten a lot accomplished so far, though, and was rather proud of myself.

I went upstairs to the small bedroom that my sister and I had shared as children. I wondered if the door had been closed since I left. I had been home to visit Grandma but had not spent a night here since. It was dusty and everything looked as though it hadn't been moved in years.

I opened the windows to let some air move through the room and shook out the quilt that was lying on the bed and sat down on the edge. I quickly found a comfortable spot and lay back.

I looked at the ceiling thinking about the day and the events that had ensued. I still couldn't believe that she was gone. I felt the tears forming again as I rolled over and hugged the pillow. The dust in the old linens filled my lungs as the tears fell drop by drop. As I fell asleep, I had never felt so alone. I cried from the misery of missing all of my family, dead and alive.

CHAPTER TWO

DREAMS

 My dreams took me to a carefree time when my grandparents were both alive and my mom had come to visit. Seline and I were playing out in the yard. We were covered in mud from the pies we were making. It was completely blissful, and the smell of the lavender that Grandma had planted around the yard felt comforting as the wind gently blew its soothing scent around us.

At one point I was certain that I saw the dark-haired lady from town standing at the edge of the tree line watching us. I didn't really pay attention to her though. It was as though she was there and may as well have been part of the trees that surrounded her. My young mind saw but just accepted it and went on.

I was pulled from the dream by a sense of something dark and sinister. Maybe it was all part of the dream, I really couldn't be sure. The scraping on the old wooden siding may have been the wind or just my imagination, but it nevertheless woke me.

After living in town for so long the night out here in the country seemed darker than it had when I was younger. I felt a shiver run through me as I let my feet find the floor. It was an odd feeling. I had never been scared here as a child. I had always known that it was safe. Of course, Grandma was a big part of the safety that I had known, and now, she wasn't here. I was really letting my imagination run wild and knew I simply must gain control. I sat on the edge of the bed for a moment letting my eyes search the darkness. As they adjusted to the night I realized there was nothing there. There was nothing but the feeling of the creepy darkness. I pulled my mind together and decided that I would not allow myself to be scared as I stood up and took a step.

I felt the breeze that seemed cooler than July rushing through the window I had opened. The old windows were heavy, and the ropes that they slid along were swollen with moisture. As I pulled down with all of my weight, I looked out, and the moon in the sky seemed shrouded by the clouds. I thought I saw a shadow in the tree line at the back of the house, but then it was gone. I was quickly reminded of my dream and the dark-haired lady. Her face was clear in my mind. Yet I didn't feel the same nonchalant feeling from this shadow. I felt a shiver run up and down my spine.

I really had to get a hold of myself. I kind of shook my head and laughed to myself as I pushed the old window the rest of the way shut, as I thought that it must have been my imagination.

As I descended the stairs that led back down into the hallway, I realized I needed to close all the windows and the doors I had left open. The old chandelier that hung in the hallway was swaying in the breeze that the wind was creating inside the house. The light from the single bulb in it was dancing around and bouncing off the walls, and the entrances of all the rooms that led off of the grand old hall. The air that stirred was stale and damp and I couldn't ever remember smelling anything like it here before. It seemed the freshness of the lavender had faded with my grandmother.

I walked through the rooms closing up the house as the rain began to fall hard. In each room I flipped the light switch but only one other bulb in the whole house worked, and it was in the living-room. I wished that I had thought to bring some more or at least a flashlight.

Grandma had always had plenty of oil for the lanterns around, so I filled one that was on a small table just to carry with me. I could hear the rain beating down on the old tin roof and blowing against the old siding as I settled into Grandma's old overstuffed chair. I recalled how she had looked while in this chair. On more than one occasion I would sit at her feet while she brushed my hair and sang her own version of a lullaby to me. I could never remember her doing that with Seline. I let that sink into my bones for a short moment. Maybe that was the reason Seline was the way she was. I had always been Grandma's favorite. She had never said that, but really, she didn't have to.

As I thought back, I knew it and I'm sure that Seline did too. I felt bad for her, knowing that at some point she probably lay in her own bed crying herself to sleep, thinking of Grandma brushing my hair and singing to me while she sat across the room watching. I couldn't imagine how Grandma could have done that to her. It really wasn't fair.

As I sat there the clock began to chime. After the eleventh strike it stopped. I couldn't believe I had slept so long. It had seemed like only moments. I did feel better after getting some rest. Even the fear that I had awakened with had subsided, and I felt rejuvenated.

I decided to get the box from the table in the kitchen and look over the books I had found. My eyes had adjusted to the dim lighting, and I thought I might be able to read them now by the single bulb and the light that shone from the oil lamp.

I took the lantern with me and set it on the counter. This would take some getting used to. It was like carrying a flashlight around only it was heavy, fluid, and much more delicate. I pulled out the bigger leather-bound book and wiped the dust from it. The cover was tattered, and the edges were very rough. Across the center of the book was scribed *Strega Secrato*.

I flipped the first page of the book open and squinted to read it in the lantern light, only to find that I didn't understand what it said: *I segreti delle Streghe solo il sangue definirà il libro.* As much as it looked like Greek to me, I honestly wasn't sure what language it was. With disappointment I closed the book, sat it on the counter, and stacked the others on top of it.

I anxiously gathered the books up and tucked them under one arm and carefully held the lantern as I walked back into the living-room. I had never been very agile, and I tiptoed to try to keep my balance. The last thing I wanted to do was drop the lantern and burn the old house down. "Hell, I bet there isn't even insurance on it," I whispered to myself.

As I settled back into the old chair I relaxed as the rain beat a rhythm of age old music with the thunder chiming in ever so often. I couldn't help but to hum along with it. Nostalgia had set in, and one of Grandma's old tunes was coming to mind, one that I hadn't thought of in years.

"Don't go out, my children. Don't go out in the night. Don't go out, my Darlings. There's things out there that bite." I hummed along some more as I recalled the words in my head.

I began to thumb through the first book, which was the smallest one of the three. The edges of the pages were tattered, and the book looked as though it had been well used. I was surprised by its contents. It was full of different recipes. These were no ordinary recipes though. They were recipes for spells. The handwriting on the pages looked as though it had been written by a child. As I carefully thumbed through the book, the pages were filled with every kind of spell I could imagine that a child may think of. At the top of each page was what it would cure, compromise, or ensure. I had to smile when I came to the page that stopped me, written across the top was, 'Keeping Mommy Safe.' As I read down the list that was needed for this spell, which was written in the same childlike manner, my jaw dropped.

Piece of mommy's hair
A fingernail to be certain
To keep the ghosts from coming in, A little piece of the curtain

Witches

A drop of two of my own blood And Seline's to seal it tight, Stir it together, light the match, And Mommy stays safe tonight.

I quickly recognized the smiley face that as a child I had drawn at the bottom of the page. I remembered now: I must have written this whole book of spells.

That was the last night we stayed with Mom. I had been so worried about her. I had overheard her telling a friend of hers that there was something going on in the house. I remembered her saying that she didn't think it was safe. At the time, I thought it was ghosts, and I didn't want them to hurt her.

I shut the book and looked around in total amazement. When we came to live with Grandma and Grandpa I never remembered it again until now. I hadn't remembered *anything* from my younger childhood before now. I never really thought about it before though, but I should have. Everyone has memories from before they are 10 years old. Now I could remember writing that particular page but not the others, but I knew that I had.

I was thoroughly confused by this. Why had I not remembered, and why the hell was I writing spells? My mind catapulted itself to another thought. I was a witch, and I would have bet money against nothing that Grandma was, too. That would certainly explain some things in my life, like my business. I had always been comfortable there with my tea leaves, herbs, and other worldly things for sale. I had always felt a kind of comfort with such stuff. Maybe it was something from my youth coming out of me instinctively.

I felt a zestful burst of energy as the questions swirled around my mind, as I turned my attention back to the book, back to my book. I began thinking of all the time I had spent with Grandma. Why would she have not told me? No, it could not have been. She was just Grandma, and something this important she would have told me. However, she was odd and she was always treating us with herbs and chants, she must have been. The bigger question that lingered in my mind was why I hadn't remembered before now. It was like it had been erased until I read that single page in that book. My recollection was still fuzzy, but I remembered writing that page.

I thumbed back through the book. None of the other spells seemed to jog any hazy memories of times gone by in childhood; only that one held something. It was the last spell I had cast, and it was rooted inside me still.

I grabbed the old oil lamp and headed upstairs to Grandma's bedroom. I had to get into her old desk. That held her most private possessions. Nobody had ever been allowed in there. I felt my spine tingle as I opened her door. I felt the urge to turn and run, but as the light from the lantern filled the room I became more at ease. The desk sat in the far corner of the room, and the chair in front of it was positioned perfectly, just as I had remembered from the few occasions that Seline and I would wander in here. Nearly always we would turn and run out together before Grandma could catch us, thinking that we had gotten away with something.

I sat and pulled the roll top up. The papers inside were neat and tidy. There in the very front was an envelope with "Kali" scrolled across it. I picked it up realizing it was my Grandmothers handwriting. She had left me a letter. I fought the urge again to cry. My mind gave way to the thoughts of her being here, I missed her dreadfully. She was always so strong and always here. I regretted leaving for a moment. Had I stayed with her, maybe I could have stopped whatever had gotten her. As the thought ran through my mind, a cold chill ran up my spine. Had I been here, just maybe I would be with her now, in the afterlife, wherever she was.

As I held back the tears, I realized that her scent had filled the room as I pulled the seal from the envelope to open it. She was never one to wear perfume, but I could not remember a time when she hadn't smelled of lavender or sage. She had a very distinct aroma, and I could smell it all around me, soothing me, as I pulled out the paper and unfolded it.

Witches

Kali,

My darling girl, if you are reading this you are surely in mourning for me. My girl, there is little for you to worry over where I am concerned. Wherever the next world takes me, I am fine. I have taken care of all that I could. There are thing far more important for you to worry about. I am quite certain that you have found the books by now and are in search of answers to your questions.

I pulled my eyes from the letter as the tears filled them.

I wanted to scream, but the calming sensation of the lavender scent that lingered in the room soothed my soul, and hushed my quivering lips. I continued reading:

Kali your sister is to never know of this letter. She would not understand most of what you will learn in the near future. You and her may have been twins but you are as different as night and day, or good and evil. She will never understand that riches are of the heart and soul, not of man. Many years ago our ancestors made their way to this land. They existed before years were even recorded. Our heritage is rich with the blood of the Strega. We were called before time to cast spells for the gods. Before humans walked the earth we had roots here.

The small burlap books were yours and Seline's when you were children. I am sorry that I had to keep this all from you. You are as dear to me as any child could have been. Your mother was not blessed with you girls' talents and was better for it. When you began to work your spells as young children, I gave you both a book to keep as your diary. When your spells were cast, life lit up. You are a powerful enchantress my dear and your sister is just as powerful, but without a pure heart. When your sister wove her web of spiders in your mother's hair, it had to stop. She had to be stopped. When you came here, I cast a spell on you both to rid you of your worries and troubles with such things. I had intended for it to last your lifetimes, and it still can. What you have or haven't remembered as of now can all go away if you burn the books. However, that choice is yours to make.

If you choose not to do that, the leather-bound book will tell you all you need to know. Your blood will reveal it to you, in the back cover lies your key.

You may choose to use this and you may choose not to. The choice is yours to make. Just remember once you have made the choice to open it, you cannot go back.

> *Remember always that I love you with all of my heart.*
> *That could not change with my passing.*
> *With Love,*
> *Grandma Hettie Marriot*

Once I had finished reading I found myself just staring at the paper. I wanted more than that. I had just learned that we had a heritage as witches, and it came with no real explanation. I wasn't completely sure if I was mad or simply astonished. My Grandma had been a witch and never told me, and also kept our own power from us, and to top it off I now had to keep it a secret from Seline. It was all a little much to take at one time. "Holy shit," slipped from my lips. I heard it aloud just as I said it. "What do I do?" I was thinking and talking out loud to myself. I couldn't make this decision.

The storm pulled my thoughts away from the letter as I heard something hit the side of the house with a loud thud. I jumped up, grabbing the lantern and headed down the stairs towards the front room. Tomorrow I would buy more bulbs and see what lights would actually work. This was really wearing on me right now. The last thing I wanted to put up with was carrying around this damn lantern.

One of the windows had opened. The old ropes that held it must have been kinked up and loosed, making the window spring open. I could not imagine it making such a bang, maybe it had actually broken inside the frame. As I hastily made my way to it, I wondered how she had put up with all this. Old houses presented lots of problems, and at her age it must have been a constant battle just to keep the house in the order she kept it.

While I was pulling it shut against the wind and rain blowing in on me, something caught my eye outside. It was the same shadow

I had seen from the bedroom window. This time I got a better look at it. I was certain it was a man or at least a human form. I did not believe it was the woman. Why the hell would it have been? What part did she have to play in this? When I blinked it was gone.

I got the same sensation of fear in my bones and thought rationally for a moment. It may have been a bear. I wondered if that was what had killed Grandma. Bears were big and strong and could easily overcome humans. If they were hungry or felt threatened they absolutely would. That would make a lot more sense than that of a creepy guy hanging around in the tree line in a storm way out in the country.

I couldn't imagine any person actually being out in this weather. Of course, there was the other idea that it may have just been my imagination. I quickly took one last look and pushed the window the rest of the way down with a heavy heave. I remembered the butter knife in the kitchen and hastily ran to grab it. I shoved it down in the side of the window frame hard and knew it wouldn't come open again. It was secure.

I sat back again in the easy chair and picked up the leather-bound book. I opened it to the back and sure enough, woven into it was a sheath that held a small piece of metal. The metal was sharpened on all sides and looked as sharp and shiny as any knife I could imagine. There was carved detail scrolling down each side with inscriptions that I couldn't read. It was in the same foreign language as the book.

I had somewhat expected this as I read Grandma's letter. I was hoping my blood was just a metaphor, but somewhere inside I knew it was not.

I imagined cutting my hand and letting the blood drip all over the book and then voila! I would be able to read this foreign language. I kind of smirked as I thought it. I had never been squeamish about blood, and the thought of that reminded me of something out of an old B movie, something completely unreal.

I thought seriously about her words as I closed the book. The choice was mine, and it was permanent, and I didn't feel as though I were in any shape to make the decision tonight. I was still tired and had learned too much to endeavor in any life changing events tonight. Besides, I was an emotional wreck. I had to sleep on it.

The clock struck midnight, and I decided to head back to bed. I wouldn't worry about the storm or any imaginary shadows lurking around tonight. I would sleep, and I would enjoy it.

The fresh linens on Grandma's bed seemed more inviting than those in my old room, so I decided to venture sleeping in there. I could still smell the lavender and sage mixed with the smell of the fresh air that they had been dried in. I turned down her bed, which had an old worn quilt on it, and crawled into it.

At some point while my mind was still fluttering I thought I could feel her with me, gently stroking my hair. I drifted off to sleep quickly and found dreams of her as soon as my eyes were shut. She was stroking my hair, singing the lullaby that she had sung to me as a child.

"Don't go out my Children. Don't go out in the night.
Don't go out my Darlings. There's things out there that bite. Don't go out my Children. There's things you mustn't know. Don't go out my Darlings. Don't run with the night crow."

At some point my dreams turned dreadful. I was chased through the night by evil demons, but I could feel Grandma with me the whole way.

CHAPTER THREE

SOMETHING DEAD

When my eyes opened I could hear the birds chirping, and the sun was shining through every crack in the room. I felt rested and renewed for the day. The storm was over, and the horrifying dreams were gone.

I lay there looking around the bedroom. The shimmering sparkles of daylight seemed to illuminate the whole room. When my eyes caught the writing desk still open I was reminded of the night before. I knew it had been no dream, no matter how much I had hoped it was. The fact of it was, I was a witch. I could either embrace it or forget it. I had to choose and despite how I wished that I could make the decision, I couldn't right now. I just didn't know what to do yet.

I got up realizing I was still in the same clothes I had worn here and decided to get ready for my day. I had left my suitcase in the car.

I walked into the kitchen to check the clock. It was seven fifteen. My attention was quickly drawn to the back door, which was standing wide open. My first thought was the shadow standing at the edge of the tree line last night. I quickly dismissed that thought and let my mind imagine a different scenario. It could have blown open during the night sometime. It was a pretty bad storm. I had latched it though, I thought. I felt a tingle in my spine as I thought of the possibilities of what could have come in through the night. I wrapped my arms tightly around myself as I walked towards it.

I stepped out the back door, released the hold I had on myself, and took a deep breath. It was a beautiful morning. The rain had rejuvenated everything. I saw a few rabbits in the tree line scurrying around, as I scanned it intently. The only difference I could see was the grass looked greener than it had the day before. There were no signs of anything out of place that I could see.

I walked around the side of the house to get my suitcase from the car. Where I had heard something hit the house there was a small limb. It must have blown out of the nearby walnut tree, and I was sure anything hitting this old house would make a terrible noise. Once again, I had to laugh at myself for being so spooked the night before. This was the safest place I had ever lived, and I was surprised at how easily I had let my imagination get away from me. It was quite funny and preposterous to me. At least I was busy trying to convince myself of that.

Whatever pack of half-crazed wild animals that had lately killed my Grandma and the other innocent people was surely long gone by now.

I pulled my suitcase into the house, up the stairs, and began unpacking it in Grandma's room. I hung up my black suit on the back of the bedroom door, for tomorrow. I only pulled it out of the closet for funerals. I put my toothbrush in the kitchen and then decided that whether I liked it or not I would have to make a trip to the outhouse.

I had always been amazed that Grandpa had converted the old oil chandeliers into electric ones and installed outlets for plugging in a few things, but had never put in a bathroom. The well was there, and the kitchen had a sink with running water from it, but there was no bathroom. I'd always thought of that when I had considered spending the night and opted not to. I liked taking hot showers in the morning, and I really did not like the outhouse, and it had always just been easier to go home.

After tromping through the taller grass around the small building and back I drew some water in the wash-pan that sat next to the sink. I also poured a little into a cup for brushing my teeth. I didn't have a fire going so it would be cold but that was okay. It would be better than no washing at all.

I scrubbed all the necessary parts and brushed my teeth, then pulled on a pair of jean shorts and a t-shirt along with some clean underclothes, which I had grabbed out of the suitcase. I automatically felt better.

I looked at my cell phone to see if I had any calls and sure enough I had. Only one, and it was from Seline. The voicemail was quick and to the point, "Kali, I wanted to be certain that you knew there is nothing I want from Grandma's estate. I contacted Tanner Button's office and had him draw everything up in your name. I will be in touch soon." After a short pause, she added with a strained voice, "Call if you need anything. Bye."

I wasn't surprised that she knew that I wouldn't call her for help. I would handle it on my own. It seemed that we only talked at holidays and on our birthday anymore, and I hadn't seen her since she moved to Chicago six years ago.

I decided I really wanted coffee. It was part of my morning ritual, and although I had thought I would be okay without it, I grabbed my purse and headed for the car.

As I drove into town I decided on going by Mr. Button's office to find out what all Seline had told him, but not till after I stop at the café to get a cup of coffee to go. I plugged my cell phone into the car charger as I drove.

I pulled over as I passed the Cater's farm. Denby and Gladys were both out by the road looking at something in the ditch. "Hey there Mr. Cater, Mrs. Cater. Is everything okay?" I said through my rolled down window.

"Oh my, honey, we haven't seen you for quite a while. We are so sorry to hear 'bout your Grammy," Gladys said with pain in her voice. Mr. Cater was still focused on the ditch.

I put the car in park, got out to see what they were looking at as I said, "Yeah, the funeral will be tomorrow at one out at Mount Point," I stopped mid-sentence as I looked down.

"Oh my God. What the hell?" I stopped. I didn't want to cuss in front of the Cater's, but the cow laying there was completely beheaded. It looked like something had chewed completely through it. The body looked intact, and for that matter the head did too, but the neck was eaten plum out.

"This is not the first one we found like this," Denby said.

"Have you called the sheriff?" I asked, not being able to pull my sight from the dead animal lying there.

"Naw, don't know what he could do 'bout a dead cow." Mr. Cater looked tired as he continued. "I figure we got us a rabid wolf pack round here somewhere. I keep my gun loaded. We gonna have to go huntin', a bunch of us, soon."

"Last night I think I might have seen a bear out by the trees. It wasn't there long though. I'm heading into town now, want me to stop and just let the sheriff know, couldn't hurt anything, right?" I asked as I turned towards my car.

"Sure, ya can tell him, he cain't do nothing, but won't hurt for him to know, I guess," he said in his deep southern Missouri draw.

"Okay, well, I sure am sorry 'bout your cows. I will see ya all later.

I need to get some coffee in me," I said as I got back into my car.

They both waved goodbye until I was out of sight. I thought about the cow and had the urge to stop by the coroner's office. I wondered if he had taken pictures of my Grandma. I didn't think I wanted to see them, but I did wonder if it was the same kind of thing that had killed her. She was being cremated, by her choice, and I hadn't seen her body. I really hadn't wanted to. I wanted to remember her alive. After seeing the cow though, I didn't know what image I would have of her. As I pulled into town I passed on the thought. I knew I couldn't look despite how I wanted to, so what was the point in stopping by?

I stopped at the Quik N Easy and got coffee. I had always liked black coffee, and today was no exception. I got the dark roast for more kick. It was hot and felt good as I sipped on it and drove slowly, trying not to spill it.

I stopped at Mr. Button's office and left a message for him to call me since he wasn't in, then made the trip to the sheriff's office to let them know about the Cater's cows. Just as Mr. Cater had said they were fairly inattentive to the situation, I guess. After all, it was just a cow.

I was on my way back home before I knew it. I let the thought of 'home' entertain me for a moment. I had roots here and did like the rural area better than the city. I could sell everything and maybe build a house at the homestead. It would be nice to keep it in the family. Or I could fix it up and get real indoor plumbing hooked up with better electric and a water heater. I let my mind wonder about things like the wiring and the plumbing and in general what all it would take to fix it up.

As I pulled back into the drive I parked and really looked at the old place. It had potential. I visualized it painted and decorated. It would be a wonderful place. I could start the farm and maybe grow herbs and sell them to make a living. I would definitely keep the thought in the back of my mind.

I took my coffee and my phone and went in. I would start back in the kitchen where I had left off. Even if I decided to stay it needed a good cleaning out.

As the day wore on, I kept myself busy with cleaning and packing until late afternoon. It was easier to just keep working, because every time I stopped my mind began racing with the things that I had to figure out.

Finally when the clock struck five, I realized I was getting hungry and as this was a one-horse town, the diner would be closing soon. I figured I better go into town and get some dinner, or I would have to settle for a can of cold tuna.

I made the trek to the diner and had them box me up a meatloaf dinner and an extra-large fresh cup of coffee to go. I was anxious to get back and work on the house some more.

When I got home I sat down in Grandma's chair and opened the Styrofoam plate. It smelled good, and I suddenly realized that I was completely famished. I had missed homemade takeout. I had become accustomed to fast food, not food like this good food. The mashed potatoes and gravy had been made, from real potatoes and broth, that very day.

As I ate it I looked at the leather-bound book on the table. It had the appearance of something newer. It didn't look quite as worn as it had in the dark the night before. The sun shimmering onto it from the window seemed to give it a fresher appearance.

As the sun began settling into its evening place in the western sky, I just sat there. I had picked over all the food in the Styrofoam box until I was stuffed and began to think of the evening ahead of me. There was still a lot of work needing to be done, and I wasn't really up for anymore of the task tonight. I had a full belly now and felt the tiring effect that it had on me.

Tomorrow I would go to the cemetery and lay my grandmother to rest. The ceremony should be fairly quick. Really her ashes were all that was left of her, and they would be affixed to my grandfather's tombstone in the sealed urn. I felt overwhelmingly saddened again. My heart seemed to ache. I had never recalled feeling so alone and deserted before. I felt as though I had nobody left.

I began to hear the drizzle of rain falling again, and I hadn't even realized it had clouded up. I let my mind wander to someplace less depressing and realized that I hadn't remembered many really wet July's here in Missouri before this year. Usually July brought an onslaught of high temperatures with very dry days and nights. I didn't like all this rain. It took away from the summer days. It turned a good 15 hours of daylight into a shorter 12 hours, and I wasn't fond of that. The only thing I could say for it was that it brought a sort of peace and melancholy with it, which evoked a simple pleasure.

I got up to throw away my trash, realizing that I had forgotten to take the recyclables to the bins and to get light bulbs. I would do that Saturday. I didn't see myself worrying with it tomorrow.

The clock on the mantle signaled that it was seven in the evening, and the clouds hovering above now masked the sunset that was imminent. I grabbed my coffee, which had cooled a bit much, and went outside to sit under the shelter of the front porch. Grandma had spent many an evening right here sitting in the old chair watching the sun setting.

I had always thought of how when the house was built the porch must have been well planned. It sat on the north side of the house. From here you could see the morning sun rise in the East and set in the west. It was orchestrated perfectly for warm sunny days. This was not one of those days. This evening was filled with rain, and there was no planning for a day like this.

I watched the rain fall. It was slow and methodical. I had always enjoyed rain somewhat. It seemed to never be pretentious; it simply was what it was, and other than cutting my days short I had nothing at all against it.

I scanned the edges of the tree line that surrounded the yard. I had to give the rain its due. In this place and time, I let go of resentment towards my loss of daylight and reveled in its calming magic. It was the most serenity I had experienced in a while, and I allowed it to fill me as I tilted my head back and closed my eyes.

The sun had fully set, and the rain had ceased before I even realized it, and I was still sitting in the old chair. The shadow coming across the yard looked surreal as it approached me. I could feel it in my spine, and I knew somewhere inside that I should fear it. I couldn't seem to muster the energy to do so, though. It was human and out in these parts, people were nice.

As the man came into my view I nearly lost my breath at the sight of him. He was tall and very muscular. His physique was slender. His hair was tied into a ponytail, and it waved behind him as he walked and fell nearly to his waist. I thought that times had certainly changed around here. There was nobody that beautiful when I lived here, and now I had seen the two couples in town yesterday and this man coming right towards me.

"Hello miss." His voice seemed slippery and hypnotic. As he came closer, I noticed that his accent was thick, and he wasn't from around here. I was guessing out east, maybe New Jersey. "My car seems to have stalled down the road."

If I would have been thinking clearly I'd have wondered why he was in the woods instead of on the road. I would have wondered why he was here at all. However, as his aura consumed me, none of the common thoughts that should have been running through my mind could find their presence.

"Well, I'm no mechanic, and I would guess the shop in town is closed for the night." There was an awkward silence as I tried to think of something to add. I had nearly sounded rude.

"No ma'am. You don't look like any mechanic I have ever seen." His smile eased the tension that had taken root in my gut.

I felt entranced by his charm. "Would you like something to drink?" I thought of my words as they came out. They didn't sound quite right to me and my insides felt like they were fluttering. I was as nervous as a schoolgirl with this stranger. And what was I thinking, offering him something to drink? I should have been thinking more clearly, but I simply could not.

His smile was wry as his eyes kept mine fixed onto them. "Yes, that would be great, thank you."

I found that I was already on my feet as I turned, pulling myself from him. It felt as though I were detaching a limb as I did so. "Well, come on in then. We will find ya something."

As we entered the house he asked, "It looks like you're packing. Are you preparing to move?"

As odd as it was, I found a comfortable place with this man and the words began to flow easily. "My grandma died, and I was just cleaning up the house." I added, "Her funeral is tomorrow." And there I was again saying more than I should. If I had been a spider I could have seen that the web I was weaving was beyond disastrous.

"I am sorry to hear that miss—what's your name?" He didn't hesitate in asking, and I didn't hesitate in my answer.

"Kali Marriot. After my divorce I took my maiden name back. Kali Rose Marriot." I knew I was saying too much—was it necessary to basically tell him I was available? For a second I was utterly ashamed of myself for my thoughts. Then I found some justification. After all, I was single, and I was a woman, a human, and this man was completely breathtaking. A book I had read so many years ago came to mind, *The Bridges of Madison County*. Could I possibly be so lonely that I would welcome a total stranger into my world for nothing more than a—

His words interrupted my thought just in time.

"Well, Kali Rose, it is a pleasure to make your acquaintance. My name is Cabe." Not many people had ever called me Kali Rose. I couldn't help but blush as he said it. It sounded so formal and polite. His eyes fixed on mine again. The blue in them seemed to mix with a black fleck and created a sphere of grayish blue that was, at the same time, electric. They calmed my soul as they looked through me.

I was sure that if there were such thing as primal attraction, we were experiencing it, or at least I was. I pulled myself from his eyes and looked down. I could feel them still piercing me as I raised my head slightly to engage them again.

"Cabe, it's nice to meet you too." I know it sounded corny, but it was all I had. My Grandma would have done the same thing. She was kind to strangers and always ready to help anyone in need. That thought made me feel a little better. Maybe I was just being nice and all the emotion from this whole event was making me a little more paranoid than usual. I was not the kind of person that would run around wanting strange men. That was absolutely it, I was just being nice. With a renewed outlook, I smiled at Cabe.

He followed me through the kitchen and the hallway and into the living room. I motioned for him to sit as I took a seat in the old chair that my grandmother had sat in for so long.

"If you like you can spend the night, and we can head into town in the morning when the mechanic shop opens. You can sleep on the couch. I will try to find you some clean blankets." I spoke hastily. Something about him made me feel comfortable, even if it was a dangerous comfort. It took my mind off of everything I was facing.

As he sat he asked "Why would you offer so much to a complete stranger?" The wry smile took his face again. "How do you know that I mean you no harm?"

"Well Cabe, I do believe I am very intuitive, and I just don't feel like you're here to hurt me. You seem like a nice enough man." As I mimicked his smile, I added, "However, I do have a shotgun, and I'm not afraid to use it."

He chuckled at me, and I chuckled with him. Honestly, I couldn't imagine being in a conflict with him. He was so tall and strong- looking. For a second I even imagined that he was bulletproof. I had to chuckle again out loud at the thought.

"So where are you traveling from? What on earth brought you to these parts?" I did have questions for this man. I also knew any answer he gave me I wouldn't find myself questioning. I had already convinced myself that he was honest and good.

"I am, in fact, traveling just to be traveling. I found myself here, I would assume because this is where I am supposed to be. Maybe, I'm supposed to meet you." His words were confident, but as they trailed off he looked towards the floor.

I knew there was more to him than he wanted me to see. I wasn't sure what, but there was more. I was intrigued. Now curiosity filtered into me and without risking being rude I simply said "that sounds very interesting. That sounds like fun."

I wanted to change the subject so I asked him, "What kind of car do you have?"

"An Audi R13." He noticed my look of confusion and added "It's a sports car. I actually picked it up in a small town, not far from here." He seemed pleased with the turn of conversation, and for whatever reason I cared.

We enjoyed pleasant conversation into the night. I told him about Grandma and my life. He didn't tell me much about himself, but he was interested and content listening to me and asking questions when I lost him. It felt good to talk to him. I was glad he had wandered here; if nothing else, the feeling of being utterly alone had subsided.

It was only after the clock had chimed out that it was ten o'clock did I even realize so much time had passed.

I showed the handsome stranger where he would be resting and pointed out the back door to where the outhouse was, and I retired to my grandmother's old room. I did grab the old worn books on my way back through the living room. I wasn't super-tired and I thought I would look them over again in bed.

I tossed the books on the bed, lit the oil lantern that sat on the table beside the bed, and changed into an old baggy t-shirt and a pair of cut-off sweats shorts.

I looked at myself for a moment in the old scarred-up, full-length mirror that sat propped up against the wall. I could see more and more of my mother's reflection every time I looked in a mirror.

My hair had taken on the same shade of red that I had always remembered hers having. It wasn't really flaming red and not really auburn either. It was just the rusty red that seemed to accompany the patina of an old worn penny.

I had remembered her eyes being just as green as mine but age and alcohol had weathered hers before she had passed, and the whites hadn't look as white. I wondered if mine would ever fade as hers had. Right now I felt myself lucky that mine were as bright as ever.

My skin, even at thirty-six, had taken on signs of aging, and

I was certain that I would get wrinkles, and they would be deep just like my grandfather's had been. I tried to keep the tanning to a minimum, only going a few times at the beginning of the season to give myself a little glow.

All in all I liked what I saw in the mirror. I wasn't overly gorgeous, just average, but I certainly had a few good points. I was very fit and kept my body in good shape, and my boobs were still perky.

I crawled into bed, grabbing the books at the same time. I pulled out the ones that I could read in the old burlap covers and laid the leather-bound one aside. I closed my eyes and thought of my grandma. I wondered how many times she had looked at these books. I wished that she were here to guide me. I had decided that I wanted to embrace my heritage and learn what I could about it. The best place to start was with my diary, the one that had been wiped from my memory until last night.

I opened the book carefully and began reading:

I not bery good at riting yet. I only 6. Gama give me and Seline this books today and I wanted to rite how much I luv mine. I don't tink she liked hers, she said it was a stupid present. I have powers. Sometimes I wish for tings and they come true an sometimes I mix tings together and it makes things happen. I tink I might be a fairy, like tinkerbell. I don't hab wings tho. Gama told me to rite those things down in my book so I dont forget what works.

As I finished looking at the page that the six-year-old me had so carefully written, I noticed that Cabe was standing in the doorway. I hadn't heard the door open, but he was certainly standing there. The flicker of the flame of the oil lantern made him look mysterious and sexy. It bounced off his bronze skin, giving his muscles even more definition than what I could have imagined.

I hadn't really noticed earlier what clothes he was wearing, maybe jeans and a t-shirt, but I certainly took notice that he was not wearing a shirt now. He had on jeans, and that was all. His chest was massive and strong. His body could not have been more perfect. There was no blemish in sight. His black hair was still tied behind him, and his blue eyes showed no signs of the gray I had seen earlier. In the lantern light they were as blue as a clear sky and were immense against the bronze in his skin.

I tried to speak as he walked across the room to me. I didn't know what I wanted to say though. I knew what I should say, 'what the hell are you doing,' may have been appropriate, but I could not find the words. I merely watched him coming closer. I had felt the attraction we shared earlier, and apparently he had also. I wanted him more with every step he took. I wanted to feel his hands touch me, his lips kiss me, and his body pressed to mine.

As he crawled into my bed, without a word, my body began to ache. I knew it was wrong how I craved him. I was caught between his cool touch that seemed like ice on my warm pulse, and the heat of the moment. I felt as though my body were steaming between the two.

His breath was as icy as his touch, but it felt good. As his lips touched mine I allowed my arms around him, to pull his cool body closer. I could feel my heartbeat quicken as his lips trailed off mine and onto my cheek. I felt his teeth gently pulling at my skin, and then he ran them along my chin. I tossed my head back to allow him to freely ravish my body. I could feel one of his hands tugging at the bottom of my shirt, crawling underneath, and up my stomach until it was fully cupped around my breast. His other hand had found my hair. His fingers entwined in my auburn locks, he pulled my head further over. His lips hadn't left my skin when I barely felt them on my neck. The icy passion was nearly unbearable. His gentle breath only broke when his tongue licked down my neck, flickering as it went. My shirt gave way to his strength as he ripped it from the neck down. I felt my body going crazy as his lips trailed down to my breasts. I raised myself as he pulled my shorts off, and then I was lying naked for him. He rose to drink in the sight of me. His fingertips gently trailed down my body as he stood and removed his jeans. The flicker of the lantern only enhanced his physique. My back arched instinctively as he crawled onto me. I could feel his desire pressed against me when all at once the whole room changed.

I hadn't noticed the aroma in the room until the light from the lantern was gone. As darkness took over I could smell lavender, sage, and jasmine fill the room. It wasn't distinctly Grandma's smell, but it was mixed with it. At the same time, Cabe jumped from me and onto the floor, landing firm on his feet.

In a near hiss he breathed to me, "I will visit you again soon, Kali." His eyes had kept their blue glow as he disappeared out the window into the darkness.

CHAPTER FOUR

A WORLD I NEVER KNEW EXISTED

All at once the room wouldn't stop spinning, and I realized I wasn't alone. The four of them surrounded the bed — the beautiful strangers I'd met in town. They were right there in my room! Fury filled my mind as this invasion took place. How could 'they' be here? I hadn't invited them to interfere with what little sex life I had, hell, for that matter, I hadn't even spoken to them.

As quickly as I had seen them, they disappeared again. "What the hell?" I muttered to myself as I pulled the blanket up to belatedly shield my naked body from the violation of my privacy.

My eyes searched to find the unwelcome guests that had been beside my bed, but they were gone. I sat up in the bed to try to regain my composure. Why would anyone break into a house just to interrupt two consenting adults having sex? Did Cabe have the mafia looking for him?

I pulled myself from the bed, found a robe to throw on, and walked out the door and down the stairs. I found the front door slightly ajar but the house was empty.

I sat down in Grandma's old chair and held my head in my hands as I let the tears stream down my face. I had endured enough. I didn't know what the hell was going on, but I didn't want to have to think of it or feel it anymore. The sadness of my loss was more than I could bear. I couldn't take anymore right now. I found myself wishing that my pulse would stop. I wish that I could be with Grandma right now. I wished that I were dead.

I had no idea of what I had gotten myself into and wasn't sure I wanted to know. What I was certain of was that whatever it was I really needed to know what was in that book. I knew that was the answer and knew what had to be done. I stomped back upstairs, halfway pouting, but most of all feeling the sickness of my life. I wanted to gain some sort of control, I had to. I felt that I was only half a person, and the other half was just lost. Maybe this would be the answer that I craved desperately.

As I touched the old leather, it was as if the book carried my very pulse. At this moment I craved it. I needed it. I wanted to know the answers. Was I crazy or embarking on a journey that would open a whole new world to me? Had Grandma been crazy also? Maybe this was inherited, a genetic disorder in the form of a brain tumor. Whatever the problem, I had to find the answer. I could not live like this. I would either find out if I was a witch, or if I were just a crazy woman. If this book didn't fix it, I'm sure there was some type of psychotropic drug that would do the trick.

I sat down at the old desk and opened the book to the sheath at the back. I slid the small knife from it and held it there above the book. I paused only for a second to consider what I was doing, then slashed the meaty part of my palm. The double-edged blade easily sliced through.

The knife was really sharp, and I had cut a little too deep, and the blood was gushing from my hand. I had never been squeamish, so the blood itself really had no effect on me, but everything else seemed to begin to swirl around me. I held my hand as steadily as I could above the book, letting the blood pool onto it until it was covered and ran off the edge. What I hadn't thought through clearly was how I would get the blood flow to stop. With my head swirling, I wasn't sure of the answer to that.

As my head spun, I felt nauseous from the blood loss or

the spirits that I suddenly realized were trying to take me over. I couldn't tell which it was, but then I could feel them pulling and pushing me around as they enveloped me in waves of crushing pressure. I instinctively knew that I had evoked spirits from before time was kept. The spirits had been swirling in the realms of the world and the otherworld for as long as there had been history. They had been the first souls created by the gods. I couldn't see their faces, but I knew they were real. I knew beyond any doubt that I had opened a new world that I was now a part of, whether I wanted it or not. I knew I had done this. There was nobody else to blame. In my human world, I had brought about a change that could not be undone.

I fought to regain my senses, but the blood continued to pour from me. In a panic I tried to get away by running down the stairs into the kitchen. Everything else that had happened before had slid from my mind. All I could think of was the blood I was losing and the spirits that seemed to pursue me.

I guess from rising so quickly along with the nausea that was swirling in my stomach and quite possibly the blood loss, after about four steps I felt myself give way to a breach in my mind. My feet quit listening to the command to stay upright. I fell. I only vaguely recall hitting the first step on the way down before I lost consciousness.

As my eyes fluttered open it took me a moment to regain my bearings. I was now lying on the couch that I had made up for Cabe. His scent lingered on it, but there were people around me. They sat staring at me. The beautiful people I had seen in town and that had been in my bedroom earlier were right here with me.

I scanned the room quickly and saw they had made themselves comfortable. Each had found a seat and was apparently just waiting for me to wake up. The woman with long silky black hair was by my side in an instant. She moved so fluidly that I couldn't quite see each step she took. It was almost as though she disappeared and reappeared next to me.

"You have awakened, my child." Her voice was as silky smooth as her hair, and her accent was thick. It seemed familiar and comforting in the midst of all these strangers. Her long slender fingers brushed the hair from my face. I didn't know her name, but she was familiar. She had watched me as a child. I remembered seeing her on many occasions, before my memories had been buried. She would help me to conjure things to put in my diary.

"Yes, my dear. I did those things. I watched over you when your grandmother wasn't there. I knew you would remember me someday." The silk in her voice matched her hair.

My mind ran wild with memories. She had been different when I was young. She had been here, but had not. I had trusted her through the childlike innocence of my youth. Her spirit had come to me any time I had needed her. I remembered her just appearing and disappearing into thin air. It had been her spirit I had seen as a child.

I reached out with one hand to make sure it was really her. I didn't want her to disappear. I needed her now as much as ever. As my hand made contact with her icy skin I realized this was no spirit, this was actually her. She was an angel here with me now. The bond that she and I shared ran through my veins, and I knew it. She was part of my past and part of my future.

I struggled to sit up, and she helped me into a sitting position. My feet touched the floor as gingerly as if they were a hot bed of coals.

I looked at the others. "Who are you all, and why are you here? This is my Grandmother's home." I spoke these words in an attempt to sound strong, but they came out weak and raveled. I wanted to kick everyone out, even my angel, as the memory of Cabe resurfaced. I hadn't invited them here with me, and if memory was serving me correctly, I was kind of in the middle of a good thing when they had arrived earlier. "What exactly is going on?" I added, putting a little more steam behind the words as I looked straight at the black-haired woman.

Witches

She looked at the others, then back to me, and then she began to speak. "I am Tarvoti," she declared. She nodded around the room as she introduced everyone else. "This is Samoda, Drake, and William." Each one nodded at me as she spoke their names.

"Your heritage has brought you here, girl, and it has summoned us." She said this in a matter-of-fact way. "You are a descendent of the Strega." With those words she disappeared, almost quicker than I could see, and was back again with the book that was still covered in my blood. She closed her eyes and smelled the book. A peaceful smile came across her lips. "You have opened yourself to the Book of Secrets." She held it up as she spoke. "You have defied your human will and taken a great responsibility onto your soul." As she continued, her words became stronger. "You must now deal with the consequences. You must choose your fate."

"I don't know what you mean. I did as my grandmother's letter said and allowed my blood to open the book to me. I was just trying to find some answers."

I found myself wanting to cry again. I hadn't done anything that would hurt anyone, not on purpose anyway. I couldn't remember feeling more like a child since I was one than I did now, in this room full of strangers who I wasn't sure if they were scolding me or not. I searched my mind to try and think of everything Grandma had put in the letter. Why had she not told me to never open the book? Why had she not warned me? And I thought of the spirits and the feelings they had pulled from me. I knew this was my fault, but still didn't want to admit it to these strangers.

The quiet broke as Samoda began to speak. "You, Kali, are not a child. The choice was yours to make, your grandmother would not, could not, have done that for you, and do not trick yourself, or us, into believing that she made this choice."

I wondered if I had spoken the words out loud that had just passed through my mind.

"No, you did not," Samoda said as gently as I figured she could. "I know your thoughts. I can absolutely read everything that passes through your mind."

The more I tried to clear my mind, the harder it became. Everything seemed to be swirling in it. I had so many questions. What do I do now? Where do I go? What exactly are the consequences? Why had they run Cabe off?

"Cabe, as you call him, had other motives for his actions." Tarvoti said.

"What, you can read my mind too?" I blurted out. I felt violated by them probing into my thoughts. "Is that something all of you can do?" I said as I looked at the two men, who were glaring at me.

Drake's eyes turned to focus on Samoda. I could nearly see the invisible connection the two of them shared. William, however, continued to glare at me. He was locked onto me, and he looked dangerously lethal. I felt him, more than I could see him. He was inside me. I couldn't stand the way he was penetrating my soul, so I pulled my eyes away to look at Tarvoti.

Tarvoti looked at me with a thick flicker in her eyes. I really thought I could see them change right before me. They were black and glossy and took on a hue of blue with black flecks in them.

"Listen, girl, I have little patience for your human pulse, so listen well. I have watched over you from the moment you were born. My soul has rendered you as part of its own. You, however, are human and very vulnerable. You can be a powerful Strega, but you have a long way to go." The anger in her voice was brutal. I knew that she could have taken my life in an instant. "You are in grave danger from Cabe. We did not catch him. William will continue to track him and stay here with you to keep you safe while Samoda, Drake, and I continue on. There is more evil in this world of yours than just right here. Your blood is what he is after—if he had wanted to simply have his way with you and be done we would have allowed it. He cannot be allowed to turn you. You cannot be allowed to fully mate. Do you understand me? You would be no more. You would no longer be available for saving. We would have no choice but to kill you ourselves."

I wanted to lash out at her. I wanted to scratch her eyes out. I was a full grown woman and did not want to be talked to in this manner, as though I were nothing more than a slut. "I would not have…" I said it as though I were in charge of defending my own honor. "…I would have stopped." Again I felt like a child being scolded, and the worst part was, they knew everything rolling around in my mind.

"You would have, but that is not the point here. I do not care if you are a slut among humans. You must understand the situation. He cannot be allowed to mate with you. You are a Strega, and the results would be devastating to all of humankind." Tarvoti spat out the words as if she wanted to open my head and pour them in. I couldn't help but think of how angelic she had seemed and how mean she was being now.

I hadn't even realized that we had all risen and were standing defensively in the middle of the room. I hadn't realized it until I looked up at each of them. Samoda and Tarvoti was at least a head taller than me and Drake and William were at least that much taller than each of them. I couldn't believe how big and strong they all looked. Their bodies were more than anything I had ever imagined.

When my eyes met theirs I realized once again, that William's gaze was piercing into me. I got a chill that ran through my whole body. I wasn't sure I wanted to be here alone with him. He reminded me of something. I wasn't sure exactly what, though. I wanted to pull from his eyes, but they held me tightly. I could envision him being my death. He would tear me limb from limb and bury me in the backyard where nobody would ever find me. I shuddered as I was able to break loose from his glaring eyes.

Samoda's voice was soft as she spoke, and I could tell that she was trying to calm the nerves of everyone in the room. "Kali," she said softly, "sit please, allow me to explain." She motioned to the couch that I had risen from.

As I sat, she took a place beside me. Tarvoti went to the other side of the room and gazed out the window. "You see, Tarvoti has little patience for humans." Her eyes caught mine as she continued. "You are in a dangerous situation right now. Your discovery of who you are was just a matter of time. Cabe or something would have come after you anyway. Your blood carries very strong powers in it. He could smell it. Your scent is strong. I, myself, could smell it from miles away." She looked up at William for a moment. "For a tracker like William, I am sure it was even stronger." William nodded in agreement. "You see, you, Kali, have been able to mask it in a larger city with lots of people around. That may have been why you have just been found, we are still figuring that out, but out here in the middle of nowhere you will be very vulnerable. That is why we are here, for your protection only. Do you understand what I am telling you?"

I wasn't sure what to say. It was all a bit much to take in.

"I really don't understand, why exactly do they want me, my blood? Was that why my Grandma put a spell on me? To keep me safe?" I was confused and lacked focus. I took a moment to let the idea stir in my mind. "Is this because I am a witch?"

I could feel the daggers shooting from Tarvoti's eyes as she turned quickly towards me. I knew instinctively what the look was for. We were not witches, but Strega. The spirits that had pursued me had let me know that the Strega are a source of power. We work in a craft that is meant for the strength of the gods.

"I… I mean a Strega? I could burn the books. I may forget it all if I do. I don't know. In Grandma's letter…"

Tarvoti cut me off. "It is too late for that. That was only an option before you opened it. You are now, what you are. You must deal with it."

As it all began to sink in I felt the room begin to relax as my epiphany took place. They did want my blood. They wanted the blood of my ancestors that coursed through my veins. I knew it was true. Yet I didn't know exactly what they wanted to use me for, and the next question in my mind was why?

Witches

"My dear girl, you have opened yourself to a world most humans will never know. I believe if you read the book you will understand more. It will hold many answers for you. Listen to the spirits, and they will guide you." Tarvoti had regained her composure, and she now spoke calmly as she walked towards me.

I looked at each of them, taking in their beauty. I could tell they were more, much more than anything I had ever known in this human world. They were all tall and lean but very muscular. Their bodies were made for war, for fighting. They looked like life and death in the dim lighting of my grandmother's living room.

As Samoda took her place beside Drake I could see their compatibility again. They were as one, and for a second I thought I could see an aura around the two of them in one color of crimson. The deep swoop of her top had revealed a tattoo on her chest. I could see the vines and only the head of what I was sure was a cherub. I wanted to ask about it, but it seemed such a trivial thing in such a time, so I looked away quickly. A smile graced her lips as she realized I was looking at her.

"You have a long journey ahead of you, Kali. For now we must go. We must track Cabe and his minions. His death will bring all of us some peace. We will leave William in charge of your safekeeping." Samoda spoke with a gentle kindness, and they disappeared into the night. I hadn't even realized the door had shut behind them when I found myself alone with William.

CHAPTER FIVE

WILLIAM

He had taken a seat in the far corner, and his lethal beauty seemed to be enough to light up the room. I hadn't heard his voice before, and I was a little surprised when he spoke. His voice was lower than I had expected and carried a tone that reminded me of distant thunder.

"You go on about your normal things. I will be close even when you can't see me."

His brown eyes were calming and seemed to ease my nerves when I looked into them. I wanted to climb into them for safety. I knew there was something about him that I could not trust myself with; I just wasn't sure what it was. It could have been the fear that I had for him. The knowing that he could and would end my life at any moment, or it could have been the attraction. He was the most beautiful thing I had ever seen. I looked away quickly to save myself the embarrassment of my own thoughts.

"Good night, William." I murmured. "If you need anything just holler."

He didn't seem to pay any attention to my words. He had turned his attention to the window that he was peering out of.

I realized how exhausted I was. I knew the events of the evening were over. Cabe was gone, and I had been saved from

49

doom and despair in the form of lust. I could feel the tears setting in before they actually materialized, and I ascended the stairs to my room.

As I lay there I knew I should read the book I had opened, I knew I should find some kind of peace with what I was before going to sleep, but I could not. I was simply tired and wanted, no needed, to go to sleep and as quickly as my eyes closed, I was sound asleep.

My dreams took me to a menacing place that night, a place where I could not escape. I did not know exactly the nature of what I was dealing with in reality, but in my dreams the vampire had rendered me useless. He had taken my guts and ripped them from me. He had twisted my existence into non-existence. The power that had once laid in me was now in him, and I was nothing more than a blood bank for him. I didn't want to live anymore. I wanted to find some kind of escape and could not. I tried to run from him and at every turn he was there draining the life from me.

Through the dream I thought I had sensed my bodyguard watching over me, but still he did not save me. My dream was half mixed with reality, and when I was finally able to open my eyes I could see that he was standing over me. His blonde hair hung straight down as he leaned over me. His eyes were a mix of green and brown in the morning light. They pierced me like knives shooting through my soul.

As I blinked to clear my eyes, of course the next thought in my head was my morning breath and how I must look after such a rough sleep. William, however, was apparently not looking at that. He couldn't have cared less what I looked like. He wasn't ogling my body in yearning as Cabe had. He was looking at something else altogether. It felt like he was looking straight into my mind.

His voice was rough, and it had taken on a near growl as he spoke. "You have a sister, a twin?"

It took a moment for his question to circle around in my mind before I could form a coherent answer. "Yes, I have a twin.

Why? Is she—" He had cut me off mid-sentence.

"You spoke of her in your sleep." His words were sad now and took an even lower tone.

I closed my eyes to remember the dream I had endured. "It was Seline, not me."

He looked at me slightly confused. "What do you mean, it was her, not you?"

"I had a dream that I was being ripped apart and was…" I wasn't sure how to go on. I didn't want to say it, but just spit it out, "…he was using her for her blood. He was feeding on her." The words disgusted me even as I said them. I held my hands over my face to try and disguise the pain it gave me to think of it.

His words were still soft as he said them, "Where is your sister now? Has she perished with your grandmother?"

"No," I nearly screamed as I finally sat up in bed. "She is in Chicago…" I allowed my words to trail off as I realized the tone I had taken with him. I didn't want to scream at him, but with the dream so fresh in my mind I didn't have a choice. It had just come out that way. "She is a total bitch, but…" I paused, "I couldn't stand it if anything were to happen to her."

He was dialing the phone he had pulled from his pocket before I had even gotten out the sentence.

"Drake, she has a sister, a twin." His voice was strong and emphatic.

My nerves returned as I watched him. The pauses between his words were daunting as he spoke into the phone. I had always hated hearing phone conversations from one end, most especially ones of life and death importance.

"I suppose that is why Samoda didn't catch it." he said, "Chicago. Do you think he knows?" Another pause then, "If she didn't notice it surely he wouldn't have either."

He turned from me, and I could barely hear him whisper, "She dreamed that she was being drained by him." As he turned back towards me he said, "No. I will keep her close, not to worry, my friend. Okay, bye."

He slid the phone back into his pocket as I looked at him waiting for an explanation of the conversation. When he didn't volunteer one I simply said, "Well?"

He looked at me. "You need not worry about this. You have enough to keep your mind entertained. Today you will lay your grandmother to rest, correct?"

That was it. I was at the end of my already-frayed rope. I leaped from the bed and began spitting words at him.

"I. Do. Have. To. Lay. My. Grandmother. To rest today. I. Also. Have. To. Worry About My Sister." I emphasized each word. "She may just be the biggest bitch in the world but I cannot let anything happen to her. And now I have to worry about something that I didn't even ask for, a blood sucking demon trying to kill off what family I have left. I did not want this. I wanted a normal life with a normal family. And further more. I still have a million questions for you! What about my children, are they safe?" I couldn't make myself stop. "You will answer my questions, you, you big ass!"

When I stopped, I found myself standing in front of him. My hands had wrapped themselves around his enormous biceps on each side. I was actually trying unsuccessfully to shake him, to rattle the answers from him. I knew he could see my anguish; you didn't have to be a psychic to see it all over me.

As I looked up to catch his eyes I saw something else.

His eyes had turned from the deep brown with the amber fleck flickering through them to a clear blue color. His face had changed as well. Teeth grew out of his mouth until fangs ran from the top down and from the bottom up. His body actually towered over me at least six inches more than before. It had become taller and leaner-looking.

"Holy shit, what the…" were the only words that escaped my breath. I didn't know exactly what had happened to him, but he had morphed right there before me into a creature that was bigger, stronger, and much more lethal looking than he had been before, and I couldn't have imagined that was possible.

I could feel him pulling from me just as I released my hands from him. Before my hands had fallen to my side he bolted from the room. He was so quick that I couldn't catch him, despite my efforts to do so.

Ironically he hadn't really scared me. Which surprised me beyond belief; he actually looked less scary than he had before. I had been caught by complete surprise yet again. Something about the creature he became stirred inside me, waking a monster of my own. It was nothing that would morph on the outside, but on the inside, I could feel it. I wanted to follow it, to caress it. It sparked a response that I couldn't deny. I followed him.

"William," I said, as I went through the doorway into the living room. He was standing by the far window looking out. I could only see him from the back.

As I stepped closer, he said, "You are as human as you are witch, you are aware of that right? You should stay where you are."

He had reclaimed his calm demeanor, and his voice was smooth once again.

"I am not certain what I am, and I am not sure what this means for me exactly."

My words had taken on the same tone as his and seemed smoother than what I had thought they would be.

As I stepped forward, he turned to me and put one of his hands up, to signal me to stop walking towards him.

"Sit, and I will talk with you. I will explain what I can."

Keeping a safe distance from me, he found a chair on his side of the room. I followed suit and sat on my side. It was almost as if a mental line had been drawn across the room. I had always been one that liked to cross lines, and I was certain that was one reason I was in this predicament now. The mental line in the room, however, was no different. I felt a burning desire to run to it and at least stick one toe over it just to see what would happen. There was something about him that seemed to draw me in.

Now, even after seeing him completely change in front of me, I wanted to get closer. Maybe it was just because I knew I shouldn't, or maybe it was the inception of my own monster growing inside of me by the moment. Whatever it was, I sat there on my side of the line and listened to William as he began to speak, the whole time wanting to cross the line. I wanted to run over to him just to be closer. It was completely magnetic.

"I am a warrior," he proclaimed proudly. "I was made to protect Nuem, my god." He paused briefly, "and everything that he holds dear, which consists of many things, but humans are among them. It is very complicated." His eyes were piercingly brown again. The amber flecks in them seemed like small stars flickering about. "More importantly, you are a Strega, a witch from days before humans existed. Your ancestors made spells for the gods to aid them in their sorcery and work. I knew some of you still existed, but with the human blood mixed within you, you are few, and even fewer of you will ever be aware of who or what you are. Just as a human trait can reoccur after many generations so can the Strega gene. I assume that is the case now. Your grandmother may have had it strongly, but your mother may not have. Just because you have it does not mean your children will. Your twin would definitely have it. You are like one. It does tend to be stronger in females than males. Does that help to answer your questions, Kali?"

I was calmer and more deliberate with my words. "Yes, it helps, but why do you think Cabe really wants my blood, and what happened in the bedroom? I mean, to you?"

William looked at me very seriously. "Your blood will empower the demon. As human as he looked I would be certain to say he has already had a good dose of it. Maybe from your grandmother or even your sister, but once they get a taste of it, it is like an addiction. They yearn for their humanity. They yearn to rule over everything. They desire nothing more than power and to destroy anything that is good. They are nocturnal creatures, and with the Strega blood they can endure many human enjoyments. I have even heard they could procreate if they drank enough blood of the Strega. They gain the partial souls of everything they mate with just as we do. With your soul comes power, and that is all he is after. Cabe, as you call him, is not what you saw. He is evil from the inside out. That is the best way I can put it to you."

"And what about you?" I asked intently.

"Ah, as I told you I am a warrior. You really should keep from grabbing hold of me unless I tell you to do so. The human blood that courses through you is hard for me to deny."

It took a moment of his words rolling in my head, 'hard for me to deny,' before I realized what he was saying.

"You want to kill me?" I blurted out. I wasn't sure how this could be safe for me.

William's eyes sparkled as a grin took his face. "No I do not *want* to kill you. I was made to destroy evil and, my dear, you have evil inside you. All of you do. I change as the warrior inside me emerges. And humans bring it out. Some of us have more tolerance than others. I try to avoid your kind as much as possible. So to answer your question, no, I do not *want* to kill you, if at all possible."

"And you think it is amusing? You might kill me, but you will try not to, you really don't *want* to. I may have been safer with Cabe."

It wasn't at all funny, but I still found myself smiling at the whole thing. I was being stalked by a killer and being protected from him by another killer. That was just my luck. I had to wonder if the whole outcome of this would be death. I really didn't see any other way around it.

William's smile was adorable. I really noticed his features, and his smile lit up the room.

The clock on the mantle chimed out nine times, telling me it was well into the morning. "Well, I guess I better start getting ready. My grandmother's funeral service is at one," I said, "Will you be

Georgia Jones

coming with me for that?"

"I will be close, probably in the woods nearby. I don't know for certain if the demon can be in the sun yet, and his scent is still strong around here. So I should stay close by."

When I entered my grandmothers room, I sat on the edge of the bed. I dropped my head into my hands and thought of all that had happened. I had really made a mess of things and hadn't done anything. How was it I could even be in this predicament? Could it be karma from something else I had done, or was this just the luck of the draw?

I thought of Cabe and the feeling I had gotten from him. I compared that to William. It was strange to me that with Cabe I had lusted after him to a point that no man had ever brought out of me. I would have done anything he asked to feel him. With William, I wanted to jump inside of him. Something about William pulled me and offered solace and protection from everything. Maybe it was just because this was all new to me, but I wanted to discover my heritage and find what was growing and raging inside me.

I pulled myself together and got my clothes off the hook that I had hung them on in the closet. I would wear my black pants and a black shirt. I thought of Grandma and how she always wore so much black. Was that indicative to our heritage, or was it just coincidence?

As I pulled on my clothes I didn't even care that I hadn't scrubbed off this morning. It was a funeral, I was sure I would get hugs but nobody would care if I wasn't exactly fresh. I was in mourning after all, and that had deepened with every event that had taken place in the last couple of days.

Maybe Seline was right in staying away. Maybe that was the line for her, and she didn't dare cross it. The dream rolled through my mind again, and I quickly tucked it away. I couldn't think of it now. I couldn't go through the pain of it again, along with the thought of burying my sister that I had grown so far away from. I thought of the other burlap book. It had been hers. I couldn't help but wonder what was written in it. I wondered if I should look. I had never been a real snoop and really didn't want to start now. She was allowed her privacy, but on the other hand, she didn't even know about it, so would it really be an invasion? I opted not to do it, at least not now.

I also wondered if my reading it would make her regain her memory of our secret childhood, and that was a chance that I wasn't willing to take. She had been dark, and I had remembered some of that. I didn't need to have to hunt her down and try and save her from herself as well as from Cabe. I would leave well enough alone for now and not touch it.

As I ran the brush through my hair, I decided I'd better wet it a little. Maybe the curls would scrunch up, and at least my hair wouldn't be too fuzzy. I would leave it down to hide the obvious circles around my eyes. As I pulled the brush through a tangle I hit my hand, and the cut that I had self-inflicted the night before came back to life. "Shit," I muttered. The crimson blood ran down my hand and began dripping onto the floor.

The door swung open furiously, hitting the wall behind it. "William," I screamed. He was in the doorway. He had been transformed. His face was screwed into a deformed, twisted mess and two fangs ran from the top down onto his lower lip and two more jutted up from the bottom. They appeared more like scissors the way they fit together. His eyes were nearly white. At first I thought he was focused on me, but quickly I realized he was looking beyond me. I turned, and as he jetted across the room I caught a slight glimpse of a shadow through the window.

The screen in that old window was gone, and the wood framed glass had been fully raised. It left the opening exposed to the outside. He leaped through it in one bound and landed, two stories down, running, chasing the shadowy creature. I knew it was Cabe, I could feel him. My human eyes couldn't completely follow all that was happening. By the time I got to the window they were at the edge of the woods.

The cut on my hand had stopped bleeding. I could see William hovering by the tree line, pacing back and forth looking for him. Then I heard a deep growl from behind me and knew before I turned that it was Cabe. "Damn, he was fast," I thought, as I slowly turned to face him. I didn't want to see him. My mind had conjured up an image of what I would face. I wanted to see him as I knew him the night before. I yearned to see his beauty. I wanted to feel his cool touch. I couldn't believe my own mind. I didn't want him to be evil, but there was nothing I could do about it.

I closed my eyes hoping, praying that if I didn't see him I would not feel him. I knew he was going to kill me. I knew he wanted to use me and despoil me. I couldn't help but open my eyes. He wasn't a monster with green goo dripping from his teeth, or an alien creature that had morphed from beauty to something demonic looking. He looked like Cabe, the beautiful man that I had almost made love to the night before.

"I am not here to kill you, Kali, despite what they say. If I had wanted to kill you, you would be dead." His voice was nearly as silken as his hand had felt on my skin. Then, in a second, he was gone.

I turned back towards the window to see William jump back through it. I stood frozen.

As William reached out his hand to touch me I felt, for a second, the same cool chills that Cabe had given me, but there was more. The ice gave way to power. I could feel it running through my pulse, giving my body a million tiny jolts. I didn't know why, but I craved it.

"What, Kali? He was in here, was he not?" As he spoke, he shook me as though he were trying to wake me. "Kali, he was in here, I can smell him."

"Yes, he was here, in the doorway."

His touch had rendered me more perplexed than I had been. The daze that I seemed to be in was nearly intoxicating.

"Did he get any…" his question taunted me. My eyes met his,

and he realized my confusion. "Did he get any of your blood?" His eyes bounced from my hand to my eyes.

I tried to comprehend the question. It was as though he were speaking to me in some foreign language that I couldn't completely understand. As his hands released me, I felt that an interpreter had just clearly stated what he had been saying, and it became clear.

"No, he didn't. He could have killed me if he wanted, right then, but he didn't."

I looked back up into William's eyes as I answered him. They were hypnotic. I wanted to be lost in them again. I wanted to touch his face, the face of the warrior that he was. I felt something I had never felt before when I looked at him. I felt the truth of love, not necessarily love itself, but the truth of it. What it was meant to be instead of what it had become.

I could feel the swirl of emotion flushing my face as I felt my legs buckle under me. I could have sworn that I had seen the stars shimmering in them as he grabbed me. He saved me from falling to the floor as he pulled me close to him. The sun could have been setting on the sea as he touched me. I would have been happy for it to last for an eternity. My blood pumped feverishly as his body pressed to mine. I closed my eyes tight, just feeling all of him.

I knew he wouldn't hurt me. His arms were those of a knight. They held me steady while my own legs still couldn't find the balance to keep me upright. His hands wove themselves through my hair to pull me even closer against the top part of his ribcage. If a heart would have been beating in his chest I couldn't have heard it, I wasn't quite tall enough.

The moment carried us both away. I heard the satisfied sound of his low growl as he leaned closer to my hair and slowly inhaled my scent. His hands pulled my hair further back as his lips found my jawline and gradually worked their way down to my neck. At first it was the cool softness that caressed them, and then I felt a hard ice that gently grazed the skin. There was an explosion inside of me. Every muscle in my body tensed as I found immense pleasure in the small prickle that had left my soul completely exposed to this warrior. As he tasted the red liquid that oozed from the tiny incision, I could feel his body tighten around me. I felt as though I would be squeezed inside of him, but I didn't care.

Somewhere in the back of my mind I remember him lifting me and laying me on the bed. I had found what I had wanted my whole life. I had found unconditional, undeniable, uncontrollable love, or it had found me.

And then, as if someone had flipped a switch, William leaped from the bed and muttered "I cannot do this."

It was as simple as that. He looked at me with sorrow and pain in his eyes. I could see the remorse in his expression before he turned from me and left the room.

When William disappeared out of the room I was left with an empty heart once again. I wanted to crawl under the bed and cry. I knew I had to finish getting ready, and I did. I was very careful with the cut on my hand. Once I had everything in place I went down the stairs and to the kitchen to find some bandages for my hand. It had begun to throb, and I could actually feel my pulse in it, but the tiny wound in my neck felt as though it were already completely healed.

I went out the front door and climbed into the car. William was sitting there waiting for me. He never looked at me at all as I drove, and not a word was spoken. I somehow felt guilty, as though I had crossed a line that I shouldn't have. However, I wasn't the one who had instigated the whole event. That was the best words I could find for it, an event, one that had repaired every break that had ever been in my heart and broken it twice as badly at the same time, all in a matter of seconds.

When we pulled up to the station, I finally spoke the first words since we had left the house. "Do you want anything while I'm in there?"

He turned to answer me, and I could see anger deep in his eyes. I knew it was there, steaming and brewing. I was hoping it wasn't directed at me, but honestly I wasn't certain. How could I be certain of anything at this point?

"No."

The way he turned up the corner of the left side of his mouth as he answered told me that he wasn't angry with me, but I could still see it there in his eyes.

After buying my coffee and briefly chatting with the clerk, who had known Grandma, I returned to the car to find him gone. I looked around for a moment then pulled away from the station, checking the clock on the dash. My day was getting away from me. It was twelve-thirty. I had to be at the cemetery in a half hour.

I made my way slowly through the street to see if I could spot William. I hated to leave him here. After all, it was a ways back to my house. When I didn't see him I wound around Dewberry Road out of town. It led straight to Mt. Point. I knew it would only take about fifteen minutes to get there, but I wanted to be there early.

I thought of William the whole way. I felt somewhat guilty that he was consuming my mind, considering I had other things that should have been worrying me, but my every thought kept bringing me back to him. What had happened at the house was special. I couldn't help but compare him to Cabe, but the difference was beyond compare, really. Cabe had made me want him. I recalled lusting after him in a humanly way. My body had wanted him from the outside in, but with William, I had wanted him from the inside out. My soul had desired him and still did.

At the gate I stopped the car and put it in park. I fumbled through the console, pulling out the breath mints and the stale pack of cigarettes that I had in there. I hadn't smoked in quite a while, maybe six months, but I believed now would be the perfect time to start again. I lit one and laid my head back on the headrest as I puffed on it. It made my head spin a little, and I let out a couple of small coughs as I exhaled on the first few drags. They tasted good and seemed to calm me, or at least give me something else to think of for a moment. I pulled each drag in deeper than the last and exhaled slowly.

I opened my eyes after finishing the whole pack only to realize that I had dropped ashes everywhere. That was one of the reasons I had quit before, they were just so darn messy. I pushed the fire out in the ashtray, dusted the ashes off of me, popped in a breath mint, and headed into the cemetery.

I drove slowly under the main gate until I saw the old truck that Dewey drove parked close to where my grandfather and my mom were buried. I pulled up behind him and parked. As I got out of the car, I could feel the tears welling again. I wanted so desperately to be a child again. I wanted to climb into my mom's lap and just have her hold me. I wanted to feel the unequivocal love of my family, and most of all I wanted to feel the innocence of childhood. The time before life really takes place, the era of our lives that we are not blamed for. I felt the pressure of a million things at once pressing on my soul and my heart.

I knelt by my mom's grave as I passed by. I kissed my fingers and put them to the ground, and said aloud, but quietly, "I love you Mom."

"You okay, Kali?" Dewey's words were soft but sincere. His voice was barely more than a whisper.

"Yeah Dewey, just missing my family is all, Grandma was really all Seline and I had left." I kept my face down so he wouldn't see the tears that were now streaming down my cheeks.

"I am really sorry. You know while yer here, if ya need anything, you can just holler at me. The wife and I would be glad to help out. I knew yer grandma and yer grandpa, they was good people."

I knew he meant it, but I wasn't good at asking for help, and I didn't expect that to change. Besides, how on earth could I get anyone else involved in what was going on around me.

"Thank you, Dewey. I think I'll be okay, though. I may just stay. I have been thinking about it a little, haven't made a decision for certain yet, but maybe."

Witches

His hand touched my shoulder as he comforted me the best he knew how to. "It would be nice to have ya around here, Kali."

I let my mind find another thought. I could fix up the old house. If I sold everything I could come up with enough money to fix it up. If only I could rid myself of the problems that had come with it, like Cabe, and the Warriors, I could make it a home again, just like Grandma had made it. I also kept the thought of William close by. I really didn't want to rid myself of him. I wanted him near me forever.

I daydreamed for a moment about what it would be like to live in the same house as him. How would that even work? He was a Warrior for God, and I was but a mere human witch. I had to smile at the thought of him going off to work slaying demons while I stayed home to cook dinner.

Dewey had finished affixing the urn to Grandpa's headstone and slipped into his truck to put on the robe he would wear for the ceremony, when the cars started pulling up. Mr. Cobb was at the front of the line, and then there was the Cater's and Mr. Button. They were followed by all the people from town that had known my grandparents. That was one thing I could say for this little one-horse town, they always showed up for funerals. Everyone who lived here knew everyone else, and even if you didn't really like them, they were still like a family. I had to smile inside at the sight. There may have been a hundred people here, all to celebrate Grandma's life.

As the people began to surround me with their condolences, I noticed at the back of the crowd I could see William. He was with the other Warriors. They made their way through the crowd and found a spot next to me. They tried not to appear out of place, but I noticed everyone looking at them, long glances that were clearly trying to figure them out.

I thought to myself, if they only knew what they really are, and just as the thought passed through me, I felt Samoda's hand on the small of my back and instantly I was calmed. I smiled at her to

63

show my appreciation for her being here. I was sad, and there was no other way to describe it, but somehow them being here with me helped.

The chairs had been placed around the other stones in the cemetery, and of course there weren't enough to go around. I sat in the one closest to Grandpa's stone, and a few of the older people sat with me. The warriors and everyone else stood, not wanting to take the chairs from the more decrepit-looking people.

When Dewey stood behind the stone where Grandma's urn had been placed on Grandpa's stone, he raised his hands and everyone quieted. "Folks, we are gathered here today, not to endure the suffering of Hettie's passing, but to celebrate her life. She was a good woman…"

I couldn't really tell everything Dewey was saying. I found myself not really wanting to listen. I knew he was talking about how wonderful Grandma was, and he would not know the half of it. She had shared far more details of her life with me than anyone here could know, and nobody could tell me something I didn't already know about her, with the exception of Tarvoti maybe. Grandma was a rock and had weathered many storms in her life, and through it all she had never shared our heritage with me. She had taken that secret with her and left it only to me in the form of a short note.

I wanted to run from this place and take her with me. I didn't want to leave her here. As the tears rolled down my cheeks, I buried my face in my hands. My heart felt as though it were being ripped from my very chest. I wanted to find the strength to gain my composure, but it was nowhere to be found.

I felt the breath on my neck before I could move my hands from my face. It smelled sweet like mixed lavender and sage. I wanted to touch it, but as I opened my eyes there was nothing there, nothing except the people that surrounded me. I looked around to find her, I knew it was her. I could not see her, so I closed my eyes tight again, and the smell was as fresh as it had been a moment before. I didn't want to open my eyes ever again. I could feel my grandmother's touch, and I could smell her scent.

The words whispered to me through the breeze, "I will never leave you, my dear," and just like that, she was gone, and left in my heart was a peace that filled part of the hole that had been there.

As I opened my eyes, I felt William's arm around me. I laid my head over onto him and allowed him to hold me. I wished that he could take this pain from me, and as he held me part of it disappeared, but only a small part.

Mr. Cater had moved and allowed William his place to comfort me. Who really knew what the townspeople thought of the Warriors? I guess Samoda and Tarvoti knew, and I am sure in their minds it was quite funny to see their reaction to them, but among us humans, who could really tell? I knew that William's touch felt good, and if I could have melted into him, I would have.

After a prayer and a moment of silence for my grandma, everyone rose. Each and every person made a point to say something to me, mostly telling me to come by, or offering help with anything I may need in this time of grief. I politely thanked them each and hugged when it was appropriate. William never left my side, and his arm never fell from around me, even when I leaned forward to hug someone.

As everyone left the cemetery, one by one, the Warriors, Dewey, and I were the only ones left. Dewey told us to take as long as we needed. He went to sit in his truck while we watched over the gravesite for a few moments.

"I heard her, she was here." I said, as if they may not believe me. "I know. She loves you very much." Tarvoti said as she gently touched my cheek with her long slender fingers. "You have a purpose now. You must help us destroy Cabe. You must choose to embrace the life you have been given."

I looked at each of the Warriors. Tarvoti wore a straight smile across her lips. Samoda wore an expression of firm hope. Drake was looking at the obvious love of his life, or should I say death,

Samoda, with admiration, and William was gazing into my eyes as though he were searching for something lost or buried in them.

The connection I felt with this Warrior was intriguing to me. My human mind told me to proceed with caution with him, but something inside me, deep inside, pulled at me, and yearned to be near him.

I turned and knelt at the foot of my grandfather's resting place and with two fingers, one each for him and my grandma; I kissed them and put them to the ground. I could feel the spark of electricity surge through me as I thought out loud, "I love you both, thank you for the rich heritage that you have given me, and I will see you in time." I rose to my feet and with William's arm around me, practically holding me up, we left the cemetery. Leaving most of my family behind to rest in peace.

CHAPTER SIX

EVIL LURKS

William got into the driver's seat of my car with me, while the other Warriors got into the Infinity SUV they had driven to the funeral. After we wound back around and through town William spoke. "Are you okay, Kali?"

I wasn't sure how exactly to answer him, so I gave him the most honest answer I could. "Well, if we are talking about my grandma's funeral, then I guess, yes. I can't bring her back, so I have to be." I paused for a moment deciding if I should go on. "If we are talking about what happened..." I had to pause again to find the words, "You know, between us, at the house. I don't know what to say. I am—"

He could see me struggling with the words and interrupted me. "I'm sorry. I shouldn't have." I could see that he regretted what had happened. "It is not within my bounds to do such a thing." He let out a heavy sigh and continued. "We have so few laws, but that is one. We are not allowed to mate with humans. How I feel about you is of no consequence. It is just not allowed."

I mulled over what he said as we drove. How could it be of no consequence? If he said that, and he did, he must have feelings for me.

"How exactly do you feel about me?" I couldn't help but say

it. I wanted to know, I had to know.

His voice was soft and sensual as he answered.

"I have never felt it before. When I first saw you I knew it was there. I could feel it the moment I first caught your scent." He paused as his hand reached over and touched mine that was resting on the console. "I cannot have you though. It is against my laws, the laws that Nuem has set for us. We cannot pursue this, Kali."

We pulled up to the house with the other warriors right behind us. As we stepped out of the car I got the distinct feeling that something was amiss. William was the only one that was still in sight. The others had vanished so quickly that I couldn't keep track of where they had gone, but I knew it was towards the house. In the sunlight William looked lethal as he circled me protectively. His claws were fully extended, and his teeth were out. His bone structure had gone from the statuesque picture of masculine beauty to the same perfection that shone through in his warrior form. I could see his muscles tense tightly in his shirt as he paced. I couldn't see anything, so I walked slowly, with him guarding me, towards the door. Unless there was an invisible monster roaming around, I was safe.

When I opened the door the stench hit me hard. The smell was atrocious. I couldn't quite put my finger on it, but it was a cross between rotting road kill and skunk, mixed with raw sewage. It was, by far, the worst thing I had ever endured.

William stayed close to me as I heard the footsteps of the other Warriors trudging through my house. I wanted to ask him what the hell was going on but decided to forgo the interrogation for the moment. I felt his arms extend around me. Their strength embraced me from behind, and I closed my eyes as I leaned back into him. He was protecting me, and I knew he could do it aptly. I could feel his breath on my neck, and I realized it was hard for him to ignore my scent. I sensed he was craving me, my blood, and I knew he wanted to devour the blood that was pumping quickly through my veins. He had tasted me, and I knew that he would restrain himself, he didn't *want* to hurt me, he didn't *want* to kill me.

My own senses became more alert, and I could hear the growls from the other Warriors. It became very obvious to me that the three of them could think as one when they simultaneously returned to the kitchen where William and I still were.

Samoda had something in tow. As she tossed it to the floor, I was held in astonishment. It was a creature: smaller framed, maybe my size or so. He was golden yellow in color, every part of him, which was easy to see because he didn't have any clothes on. He lay there completely naked. He looked almost fake, like he had been spray-painted. Even his hair was the same color. As he opened his eyes they were not much different from his body. They were golden as well, and outlined in black.

"Holy shit! What the hell is that?" was all I could say as I pulled away from William. I had never seen anything, ever, like this, and now here in my kitchen there were four Warriors with gleaming teeth and deformed bodies surrounding this creature that looked like he stepped out of a nightmare, or was about to step into one.

I let my eyes drift over to Samoda, who seemed to be looking into this creature's mind. I could not be sure, but it sounded like I heard something like a voice say, "I knew you would come." It seemed to come from the creature, but not from his mouth, maybe from his mind or his soul. His eyes were focused on me.

Then I had to cover my ears. Three of the Warriors were upon it. It felt like the thing's scream would make my eardrums burst. William joined the others, and the creature was being devoured by all of the Warriors at once until all that was left was a golden lifeless corpse of what he had been.

In a near stupor, I watched his body dissolve into a pile of goo on the floor right there in front of me, and then I watched the goo evaporate, leaving just a slight wet mark on the floor, which also disappeared quickly. There was nothing left of the creature at all, and it made me wonder for a moment if I imagined the whole thing. I realized that I had not as I looked at the Warriors that surrounded me. Tarvoti and William had returned to their former glorious selves. Drake and Samoda however were fixed on one another, and you could see the smoldering tension between them. In a moment they disappeared out the door.

Tarvoti broke the silence, "Ah, young love." The smile on her face was both happy and sad. "They have not been mated long, so every little thing makes them flitter off to consummate their unity again. I remember well the same feeling with my Charlavae. We had much more control as time passed, but the passion was as great as ever. I do miss him so."

"It must have been a great love." I said out of sheer compassion. I could tell she was in pain, and for such a strong being, she wore the pain rather openly.

"He was my only love." She stated that with less explicit emotion. Her eyes flashed from me to William. "Humans die, that is what they do. I do not wish this pain on you, my friend."

I knew that she had directed the last part at William, and he acknowledged her statement with a nod. There were so many questions that I wish I could have asked, but I chose to change the subject quickly.

"Tarvoti, what was that thing?" I directed the question to her purposefully. I wanted to change her train of thought, as if I still had some measure of control. And I was successful, at least on the surface, though who knew what was really going on in her mind? But still, she answered my question the best she could.

"Evil is what he was. He was evil from the inside out. Some sort of Quip, a combination of many different things all bred and crossed into one being." This was her explanation, and she didn't seem overly excited about it. "The Avorians are continuously coming up with new creatures in an attempt to trick us and you humans. That *thing* is another type of minion in Cabe's army. I'm sure we will see more of them."

"I have never seen any creatures until now." I said, not really challenging what she had said, just letting her know that it wasn't a trick for us if we hadn't known about it.

"Silly human, that is part of the trick. Usually you don't see them, and if you do, you could not have the strength to kill them. They would kill you, and then who would you tell?"

After a quick pause to let that saturate my mind, she added, "Exactly! You wouldn't tell anyone, so nobody else would know. Something has been killing you all off in herds lately. Just like your Gra—" she stopped mid-sentence. Even though I knew what she was saying, I didn't want to hear it, and she was kind enough not to finish. "That thing right there," she pointed at the empty spot on the floor where it had lain, "could have been the culprit."

I knew Tarvoti was right, but before I could agree Drake and Samoda came back through the door into the kitchen.

With all of us back together it didn't take long to realize that we would be getting down to business. The Warriors had a common goal to focus on, and somehow I felt privileged to be included. I wanted Cabe dead and gone as much as they did, especially after realizing that it could have been him that had actually killed my grandma.

William had taken my hand and practically dragged me into the living room, where he sat next to me. Samoda and Drake were close behind us and sat on the loveseat across the room. Tarvoti appeared soon afterwards with my books in her hands as she took a seat in Grandma's old chair. I felt kind of funny seeing her sit there. I had only ever seen Grandma there before I had taken over her place in the last few days. I guess under the circumstances it would be completely inappropriate to squabble over such trivial things, and besides I really was completely comfortable sitting next to William.

I almost felt as though he were "my" Warrior. With that thought, Tarvoti and Samoda both looked at me with an unkind gleam in their eyes. I knew they knew my thoughts and were unhappy with the one regarding William. It really seemed unfair that they knew what I was thinking.

"This book does speak of demons drinking the blood of the Strega to allow them to bear children." As Tarvoti closed the book she looked down as though she were seeing through the old wooden floors. "There is a spell to prevent their reproduction but nothing to stop the actual mating."

"It would be a good place to start. We don't want her to end up…" William stopped. I would tell by his expression that the thought of it was tormenting him.

"I do believe that is what he is after, think of it as half Strega, half demon. They would be very powerful," Samoda clarified, as though she had experienced an epiphany. She rose from her seat and paced to the window. "If he could mate with you, not kill you, but have you bear his children and raise them in the human world, he would soon have an army of Quips." She turned, looking insightful, and added, "like the one we destroyed in the kitchen, only I'm certain that they would not be recognizably different from humans. That creature reeked of many things. I could even identify some of the demon-dragon in him. Vlad."

Samoda turned to face me, and even though she was across the room from me I felt like she was right there in front of me, maybe even inside me.

"You girl, are the key."

With those words I knew that she had heard the Quip tell me that he knew I would come. I had to defend myself.

"I did not know him. I have never seen anything like it before, ever."

"I know you don't, but that is just further evidence that you hold the answer."

She turned her attention to the other warriors. I knew they were having their own silent conversation about me. Then Tarvoti spoke up.

"No." She looked at William. "There would be no good in that."

I had the distinct feeling they were talking about killing me.

I couldn't be sure, because I had no clue what they were thinking, and once again, I felt violated.

"I think I am going to go change and lie down for a while. I didn't get much sleep, and I am feeling very tired." I really just wanted to get away from them all.

I went to Grandma's old room. As I opened the door I could feel the breeze from the still open window and walked over to close it. I thought for only a moment about the events that had occurred in here earlier with William. Then out the corner of my eye I saw her shadow.

It was my sister! I jumped backwards, nearly knocking myself and the bedside table to the floor. I couldn't believe my eyes and was in complete and utter shock that I was seeing Seline standing there.

In a whisper I said, "What the hell are you doing, Seline?" I grabbed her tightly in a hug. "Why are you up here? How did you get—"

My own thoughts interrupted the sentence. She looked confused. Her unfocused expression sank into my head. Something wasn't right with her. How did she get here? Where was her car? Why was she hiding up here?

Suddenly I knew it wasn't Seline. I wanted to let her go, but instead I kept my arms wrapped around her as I looked at the desk that was still open. The knife that I had never returned to its sheath in the back of the book was lying there.

I could feel her changing right there in my arms. I wasn't certain what it was that I had a hold of, and it was really creeping me out, but I did know for certain that it was not Seline.

I couldn't help but think that it would be a great time for the Warriors to make their entrance—and then it spoke. The hissing sound that came from it was hard to understand, but the words came through. The noise it made caught me off guard, and I let go. I inched my way to the open desk it, keeping my eyes glued on it.

"He sssaid you would come. He sssaid you would sssave

ussss."

I surveyed its changed body, and it was just like the thing in the kitchen. It was now completely naked, completely golden, and obviously male. I wanted to scream out, but couldn't. I didn't want to alarm this thing, so behind my back I felt for and finally found the knife. I held it in my hand.

I watched it slowly change back into Seline, and continue speaking.

"Isss thisss better? I don't want to ssscare you."

I didn't know what to say and for a moment I was taken in by it. I couldn't attack my sister and stab her, even if it wasn't really my sister. It looked too much like her.

"Why do you look like Seline? How do you know her?" I asked in a hushed tone. I wasn't sure why. It would have been fine for the Warriors to come in and destroy this thing to save me from having to.

The creature cocked his head slightly as though it didn't understand the question. Then it hit me. It didn't look like Seline, it looked like me. I charged!.

I was on top of it, my knife slicing through its body like warm butter. It screamed! The Warriors responded instantly. The door opened with a heavy thud as my Warrior burst through, and then I was caught in the middle, between the Quip and William. I could feel the creature squirming underneath me and William's weight on top of me as his teeth tore through it. Once again the scream felt as though it would make my ears bleed. It was the highest pitch noise my ears had ever endured, and I couldn't cover them. My arms were trapped in the struggle.

Moments later the creature under me began to turn squishy, forming a pile of goo. I could feel it penetrating my clothing until it finally reached my skin. I felt a million spiders biting me all at once, and it was as if it were pulling me into itself. It was grabbing at me, trying its best to suck me into the everlasting darkness.

William grabbed me up off the floor and even his cold hands

could not relieve the stinging that had taken root in my body, from my backside to my shoulders down to my toes. Every place on my body that had touched the goo was on fire.

The other Warriors were here. Each looked like they had rehearsed this scenario a thousand times from the way they reacted. Tarvoti took her spot on her knees on the right side of the bed, closest to me. Samoda sat on the left side of the bed within reach. Drake stood by the door with his back to us watching for anything, and William went to the window to look out.

"*Sca La Tre Du. Secco Du Lat. Secco Du Lat.* Woden, I summon you now to our aid." Tarvoti's words seemed to summon something to the room. A wind was coming from within.

Whatever she was doing wasn't helping. The burning on my back seemed to worsen. It was spreading all over me. I could feel its fingers creeping around and onto my ribcage.

The burning pain grew worse. Even the clothes I was wearing were melting with the acid of the demon, clawing and biting the life out of me. But Tarvoti's wind was stronger now, a whirlwind that bore me into the air. I felt a small, a very small, degree of relief from the pain as I was lifted from the bed. That lasted until the tornado-like force that had consumed the room began to tear at my already tender, blistered, and ripped skin.

CHAPTER SEVEN

ATHERIA

The wind held me fast in place, and I could barely see the Warriors around me. It continued to buffet me until the rest of my clothing was ripped from my body. I was completely nude, in the middle of a cyclone that seemed to be sandblasting what skin was left on me. The pain was more excruciating than any I had ever imagined in my worst nightmares.

As I prayed for death to take me away from the scorching agony, I was released. It didn't come gently or softly. I felt like I was dumped onto the ground from ten feet in the air. As my eyes blinked shut, I found the numbing silence all around me, and I chose not to open them. I could feel life itself slipping from me, and I was okay with it. It was taking me away. I would have been happy to escape forever what I could not endure.

I opened my eyes with a jolt. I expected to feel the same torment as when I had closed them. Instead, I found that it was better. Not gone, but better. I was lying in what felt like a cloud of feathers. They were soft and comfortable against my skin.

As I looked around realizing my surroundings, I was not surprised. At this point, was there anything left to be surprised about? I had experienced many things lately, and this was just another of those experiences. The bed that I lay in was grand. It was very large, bigger than a king size would be. The posts were carved ornately and jetted up to the ceiling, and delicate lace hung down around them. The furnishings were elaborate and looked like they belonged in a museum or a mansion. The candelabra that hung from the ceiling in the center of the room was golden, and each of the holes were filled with a bright red candle. The cascade of sheer curtains that blew along one whole wall seemed like billowing ivory. The massive pictures that hung on the walls were all scenes of fairies, elves, and tiny humanoids. The mirror on the wall opposite the bed caught his reflection, and my eyes stopped to admire him.

"You're awake, Kali." William sounded sensual and soft. He was positioned at the head of the bed on my right. The chair he was sitting in was as ornate as everything else in the room. It was red with golden accents in the carvings on each arm. It was large and fit William nicely.

"I didn't know if you would awaken or not. Nuem said you could die. The trip alone is not made for humans, and with all of your other injuries... We didn't know."

His hand stroked my hair gently. A pulsating shock ran through me, and I moved slightly, bringing back to life the stinging pain in my back. He sensed my discomfort and moved his hand away quickly.

"I..." My voice cracked, and I felt very weak. "Where am I?"

"You are in Atheria. It is the homeland of our God, Nuem."

I closed my eyes to try and remember anything. Everything beyond the tornado was a void. I recalled landing and hurting so badly, then nothing. I thought death had taken me away.

"Atheria? And I'm not dead? What is going to happen to me?" I had a million questions running through my head as the door opened and Tarvoti appeared.

"You are not dead." Her words nearly verged on disappointment. "Nuem said no human has ever survived the trip before. You are the lucky first."

I hadn't noticed her accent as much as I did now. Every word she spoke was thick, and at the same time hypnotic. She seemed so far from the angel of my youth. She was harder now. The scars that riddled her skin didn't detract from her beauty. She was hard and calloused from too much life, or I guess it would be better said as, too much death.

"You, go now. I have work to do here." She spat the words at William and waved her hand to emphasize her seriousness. He obeyed quickly and exited the room without as much as a goodbye.

"What are you going to do to me?" I really didn't want to know exactly, I just didn't want to be caught by surprise if she began hurting me.

She approached the bed so quickly I didn't see her move. She began speaking at the same time.

"The fruit from the forest is what has saved you. I am going to rub more of it on your back. Now, can you roll over, or should I do it for you... again?"

"Oh sorry," I said quickly. I felt kind of bad that she had to double as my nurse now, and she had a way of enhancing that feeling. "So you saved me?" I said as I rolled onto my side, very gently.

"Well. I wouldn't say I saved you, but I did pluck the fruit and begin rubbing it on you. William actually carried you here. I don't think I have ever seen a Warrior run like he did with you in tow." She kind of laughed as she said the last part.

I winced as the fruit hit my skin. Anything touching me right now hurt. I wondered what it looked like then got a horrible image of bubbled skin that was peeling away from my body.

"Do you want to see?"

I turned my head as far as I could to make eye contact with her. I didn't have to tell her my confusion, she already knew it.

"Do you want to see your back? Oh damn. I know you do."

She seemed in a fairly testy mood. She grabbed me and rolled me over to be facing her, and at the same time reached down to her own wrist, extended her fangs, and made a small incision in it. She held it to my mouth and offered me a drink of the blood that was now dripping from her.

I wasn't sure if I should, but I couldn't refuse. I had tasted blood before, but only the occasional cut that you instinctively put in your mouth and then want to spit out because it leaves a taste of an old dirty penny. We have all done that.

This blood however smelled like sweetness. I wouldn't say honey or ice cream, but sweet like honeysuckle that is ripe on the vine. The smell that is always better than the actual taste.

When I put it to my mouth many things happened all at once. First it was good. I didn't want to let it go. I closed my eyes to savor the flavor that it produced, and I found that I was actually sucking instead of allowing it to drip. Second, my mind came alive. I could see things, different things. I craved something, but wasn't sure what. I could see the invisible pores in her skin as I sucked feverishly.

Then she pulled away from me. I looked up at her. She looked different. I noticed that her eyes were full of many colors. They were for the most part bluish violet, but they also had little flecks of every color in the rainbow flickering through them. She rolled me back over onto my side, and then I was seeing through her eyes.

I could see my own back. It was blistered, but not like I had thought. It looked more like an acid burn. The skin was charred and purplish, but it didn't look like what I had pictured.

"Wow," were the only words that would escape my lips. In this world where anything could happen, this was really happening.

She rolled me back over onto my back. Her quickness was unimaginable, but I could see her every move now. Still, she was on top of me before I could even resist. The instinctive fear of death sent a chill through me, and then I realized I didn't want to struggle. She had pulled my head back and in the same motion, dove into my neck with her lethal fangs. I could feel every sensation in my body go wild with excitement. As she pulled back to release me, I found that I didn't really want her to stop, but she did.

"There, you should heal much faster, and you should be easy to keep track of."

She said it as though it were a job for her. I was somewhat saddened. It had been an emotional experience for me. I was looking straight at her, and her lips never moved as I heard her speak.

"It was planned. Nuem had instructed me to do so. You will be much stronger. You will be able to endure these events more easily. I did enjoy it though. You are very tasty."

Her laugh was much lighter in her thoughts than it was when it was aloud.

"So what will this mean for me?" I thought, and a picture of William entered my mind.

She quickly cut me off with her actual words. "That is between you, William, and Nuem. He will be in shortly to see you. I cannot say his thoughts on the matter. The only thing I know for certain is that no warrior has ever been allowed to mate with a human." As she turned and began walking towards the door she added in her thoughts, "but, no warrior has ever wanted to."

She looked back at me as she walked out. I could still see her, though. The hallway was lined with mirrors and as she walked down it, each time she glanced into one I saw her reflection.

I could see deeper into her than most would have wanted. I could feel the pain that she felt, and it was horrible and fresh. I knew it was constant though, and had been there for as long as her mate had been gone. It was gnawing and never-ending.

I could also see her thoughts of me. She thought of me as a child. When she looked at me she saw me as the young girl that she had helped conjure up spells and such. She had been tasked with setting her spirit free when she had found me as a human child and had never really let me go. Even when she wasn't there she worried over me. I thought of how endearing that was. I was kind of like her own child that she had never had as a human. I could see all of her… As a human she had been much like she was now, only her work and her loss had hardened her. Her beauty was insurmountable. I felt like there was nowhere she would be able to go and escape me, and I liked it.

Then her mind went as dark as it had been before, but I was not alone for long. Moments later the door opened. He glided through the doorway and turned to shut it behind him. He was at least eight foot tall. His waist-length hair was primarily golden with black streaks running through it. When he turned toward me his face was many things. It was chiseled and masculine and his eyes, oh those eyes, were those of an angel. One was as dark as night and the other as light as a bright clear sky and that was what they each reminded me of, day-time and night-time. His ears were pointed up at the tips of them. The only other thing that I was able to observe was the crimson robe that trailed behind him as he appeared at the edge of my bed and sat down.

I was busy watching him with cautious admiration when I heard him. His voice rang through my head as though it were being poured in through my eardrums.

"You are a strong human woman, Kali." His lips never moved but turned up a smile on one side. I could feel the compassion he emitted stroking me gently. "I understand why William adores you so."

"I, I…" I didn't know what to say and pulled my eyes from his and looked down towards his hand, which had reached out and was resting on my feather-covered calf.

"You need not worry. I am not angry. I was merely admiring your strength. You have the heart of a Strega Warrior, much like my beloved Tarvoti. Of course, you know that you are half Strega."

He waved his free hand above his head, and the candelabra came to life. The flames of each one flickered and danced in the air for a moment before they stilled themselves and burned low but brightly.

"Does your back feel better?"

I hadn't expected to see his lips move as I heard the words. "Ah, yes. Actually, it does."

I kind of wiggled a little in the bed, and it didn't hurt at all. I was surprised that it felt as though it had never happened.

He rose slowly from the bed and glided to the smaller open doorway across the room. I hadn't even noticed it before. He entered it and emerged quickly with a green cloth draped across his arm. He was back to my bedside laying the dress out for me.

"You will look ravishing in this." He moved to leave the room, only to turn back to me. "We are having a party tonight. I think you will enjoy it tremendously."

With a smile he was gone. As he made his way down the hall I could hear Tarvoti's thoughts re-enter me.

"My dearest Charlavae, how I miss you so."

The pain in her heart was nearly unbearable for me. I couldn't imagine what she herself must have gone through all of these years without him. She saw me probing there and clearly sent me a message.

"Love only breeds heartache, and our love aches for all eternity."

I rose from the bed and was truly surprised as I twisted and turned my body that my back felt so much better. Not only was it better, there was no pain at all, it was completely healed. I turned to look at it in the mirror and was again pleasantly surprised that it looked like it wouldn't even scar much. My naked body was practically glowing with perfection.

I picked up the garment that Nuem had laid on the bed, and as I stepped into it and pulled it up I could feel myself changing. I felt like a princess. When I turned to look in the mirror at the emerald flowing material my breath was nearly taken away with astonishment.

It felt surreal. I could have been a character right out of a movie! I held the two strings around my neck to tie them as I looked down. The material clung to me to the waist. I could feel the back was dropped low, nearly to my tailbone. The dress draped and billowed out from the hips. About the knee line there was an addition of white lace that had black spun through the ends, it wove its way through the green sea and peeked out like waves against a calm emerald ocean.

My eyes moved upwards to find my own face. It too had been transformed. There was not a wrinkle or speck on it anywhere. My eyes were as green as the dress. My red hair had brightened and looked fresh and kind of tussled. I was an image of beauty, even if I did say so myself.

"Oh, please, get over yourself."

The laugh that came afterwards made me feel slightly ashamed. I knew Tarvoti was making fun of me in her own lovable way.

Even so, I was glad to hear her. "Are you ready?"

I am not certain that I even realized that she was in the room with me. She was standing at the door waiting for me. She had one hand on her hip and the other on the door knob. She was anxious for whatever was going to happen.

"You will find out soon enough." she whispered in her mind. She knew I was anxious also.

"You do look scrumptious though."

Her tongue flickered across her teeth as though she were talking about a big juicy steak or something delectable. I only smiled at her, because she had her chance. I was certain that if she were going to eat me, she could have done so many times before. I felt safe with her.

I picked up the front of my dress and exited through the heavy wooden door she was holding open for me. I turned and waited for her as she closed it and let her lead the way.

As we made our way through the labyrinth of hallways I was certain I couldn't find my way back on my own. Around every corner I found a new adventure waiting. There were giant paintings, elaborate mirrors, ornately-carved posts and trim moldings, and large intricately-detailed single and double doors.

Witches

Finally we came to a hall with a large archway at the end of it. Inside it was dimly lit, but a light flickered gently from within. I could hear the music that awaited us. It carried a heavy bass beat that I could feel surge through me. The buzz in Tarvoti's head became louder as we got closer. I could tell there were a lot of people already there.

Tarvoti's hand squeezed mine as we neared the end of the hall and we came to a stop.

"None of these creatures will hurt you, but you should be prepared for what you are about to see. If you are ever in fear I will know, and I will find you."

The smile that she gave me with her words was as gentle as my own grandma's had been. I felt comforted by them, but I couldn't imagine being scared here in such a place of peaceful bliss.

"Thank you, Tarvoti."

I squeezed her hand back, and we continued through the doorway. I looked down momentarily to be sure that my bare feet would navigate the single step while holding my dress up in the front. The last thing I wanted to do was to trip my way into the party.

The scene was surreal and something that would have come straight out of a fairy tale. With each step the cold stone on my feet became warmer to my senses. Tables were set up with fruits piled onto trays of silver, and others held large bowls that steamed. Everything smelled like honeysuckle and perfectly aged bourbon. Red material draped the exterior. It had been meticulously placed to drape around the edge. I followed it with my eyes to the front part of the garden, and there stood a large chair sitting up on a stage. It was all made of the same stone. Trees jutted up in the corners of the whole garden area. Their plumes, which looked like giant feathers, danced to the beat of the music and took on the light of the small fires that jetted up from the torches that had been lit about every 10 feet around the arena.

It was hard not to notice the creatures that flitted around.

There were little winged creatures flying about. They seemed to be playing tag. Their laughter was so high pitched that I wasn't certain that it was coming from them or some altered breeze in the distance. Their skin was nearly translucent, and I was sure that I could see the blood pumping through them each time one slowed enough to let me get a good look at it.

"Serephine." Tarvoti thought. I knew it was directed to me with the tone of her thought.

There were some small round creatures that looked kind of like miniature men. They were all busy looking. A short husky lady was straightening what I assumed to be her man's shirt collar and scolding him over something. They all had the same sturdy, stout features.

In a large group at the far corner of the garden a group of creatures had gathered together. These beings were beautiful in an odd sort of way. They each had very long golden hair that was combed straight back. Their ears jutted up towards the sky, kind of like Nuem's did. They wore items of forest flora such as vines, leaves, and brush for clothing, and it was all in browns and greens.

My eyes found the Warriors. They were all together talking in a group made up of smaller groups huddled together. William's eyes found me and never left as Tarvoti and I slowly continued on, taking in everything. Tarvoti was kind enough to not leave my side until we reached the group of warriors, where she kind of handed me off to William.

"Stunning," was the only word that came from his lips, but if his eyes could have talked, I know there would have been so much more. He was looking at me with longing and desire when moments later, the party completely stopped.

Every being in the garden looked towards the same archway that we had just come through. Silence overtook the audience, made up of all the different creatures, as Nuem walked through and made his way to the stage. I felt his eyes on me for a short second as he passed. When he took his place on the stone stage at the front of the garden, he raised his hands and spoke cheerfully.

"Children," the crowd of beings roared in gleeful response at Nuem's single word. "We have a special guest with us this evening, a human."

Everyone quieted as they turned to look at me. William immediately draped his arm around my shoulder and held me close to him in a protective manner.

"Everyone, this celebration is special, so on with the party. Drink the Noi. Eat the fruit. Enjoy what the Serephine and the Animae have prepared for us."

As the music started everyone resumed the party. I watched as they poured steaming liquid they called Noi into goblets and sipped and as they took bites of the fruit that I was certain was the same fruit that had saved me.

Tarvoti was near me as I heard her thoughts. "Come now. You and William come with me now." She had such power even in a mere thought! I tugged at William and motioned for him to follow me as I followed her, trying to keep up. Her black dress flowed behind her, allowing me to keep track of her in the crowd. We wound our way through the party until we were standing in front of the stage where Nuem sat, smiling down at us.

"Paela." Nuem summoned the little Serephine that was flittering by. She flew up to him and stopped attentively.

"Paela, will you get something to drink for Kali? Remember she is human."

She flitted away as quickly as she had stopped, then swiftly returned to land on the table closest to us. She was carrying a cup that looked like it weighed more than she did. It was silver and looked bigger than the ones everyone else had. I could see that it was empty.

I looked at her more closely and realized she also had a small knife, similar to the one I had used to cut my hand, only smaller. Before I could say no, she had swiped it across the back of her own little hand. It took only a moment for the liquid to flow from her.

It filled the cup quickly and looked as clear as water. As it touched the silver it turned deep blue and appeared to thicken. I looked from her to the cup until I was certain that her small body would be drained.

"Please stop, I'm not thirsty." I wanted her to stop immediately. I wasn't about to drink the blood of a fairy or Serephine or whatever she wished to be called.

She did stop, but not until the cup was about three-fourth's full. The little squealing giggle that came from her with her words was like that of a child, and I immediately felt guilty shame that she would do this for me.

Her dainty face took on a slightly pinker shade, and she looked at the Warriors and then back to me. "Do not worry, Miss Kali, this is all that I am certain would be safe for you to drink here. It did not hurt me, and there is more where that came from if you like it."

"No, no, this is plenty. I'm really not thirsty at all, but thank you all the same." I wanted to be polite; really it wasn't every day I got to meet such a wonderful creature. She flitted to the other end of the table and sat right on it, facing us. She smiled at me and motioned for me to take a drink.

I hadn't realized that Nuem, Tarvoti, and William also now held a cup. Nuem held his up in a toast. His words were meant for William and I, and we held ours up accordingly.

"To life and death," was all he said. They each took big drinks of the Noi that was still steaming out of their cups, while I took only a small sip of the blood I was holding.

It wasn't nearly as tasty as Tarvoti's had been earlier, but it was sweet and syrupy. So I took another bigger drink.

"Tarvoti, I would like to thank you for your assistance. William and Kali, will you please follow me. I think we need to talk about some things."

Nuem waved Tarvoti away and stood. He exited the stage with William and I trailing right behind him. Once he got to the trees in the corner of the garden he stopped and began to meander about as he spoke.

"Kali, you are a human, an exceptional human, but a human nonetheless. William, you are a Warrior. It has always been a law…" He paused as he emphasized the word *law* "…that no immortal creatures are to mate with a human. I know the Avorians have not bound themselves to the *law* as they should, and it has created many, many problems. Those types of problems cannot be undone; they are bred into the race for all eternity. These things come at a very high price, one that no human could possibly be prepared to make."

I wanted to crawl under the tree. I knew what he was saying, and I didn't want to hear these words: William and I could not be together. Nuem kept his concentration on the tree as though maybe it could convey his wisdom and help him to find the words that would enlighten us to his way of thinking.

"I am devoted to you and the duty that you put before me, Nuem." William's words were sincere. "I have asked for nothing and do everything you ask of me, as completely as I can." He paused and looked to the ground as he continued. "I know I love her though. I am sorry that she is a human. I have never known this feeling before. She is the one that completes my soul. I can feel it radiating between us."

I was surprised to hear those exact words coming from him. It was as if he had known me my entire life, not just a few short days. He felt something deeper than anything he had ever felt, and he felt it for me.

"You are a good Warrior, William. I appreciate your years of service to our common cause." Nuem's eyes were now fixed directly on William. "You have a will that is your own. I have never enslaved my children. You do realize that you could kill her without even realizing it. She is a very fragile creature. And one thing is certain, *she will die*."

He stopped short on those words. They rang in my ears, echoed feverishly in my head.

"Won't we all?" I let that slip from my mouth. I hadn't even realized that I'd said it aloud until they both looked at me.

"Possibly, but for you it is certain. The body you have now will lie in the ground while your soul is set free. You, Kali, may become a Warrior, a Serephine, an Animae, or you may become a demon. That is yet to be determined by your human life. But *you. Will. Die.* And when a Warrior mates it is for eternity. Your death could kill William, if mating with him doesn't kill you. Your souls would actually mix. You would become part of him and he part of you. The reality of it is, you will become stronger, but he will become weaker."

Nuem had gotten so close that he was actually hovering over me as he finished. I found myself trying to avoid his touch by leaning backwards. I knew he was trying to drive a point home to me. I meekly responded as I looked down to avoid his eyes that were now staring through me. "Am I not also Strega?"

He finally made contact with me. I wanted to fall to my knees at his touch. It was like being electrocuted. I was paralyzed there with his finger pointed at my heart. He picked me up off the ground with the connection that he had made with my soul. I could feel the pain searing through my whole body, with no exit. It churned its way through me until I was certain that death would come for me and carry me away while in the straits of this God.

He released me and I fell, hitting the ground with no cushion at all. It happened so quickly that even William could not catch me. Nuem's voice became thunder as he held his hands above him. Large black wings began to creep out from behind him. His face warped into a form similar to the Warriors when they changed. Fangs emerged until they were curved down from his lips, and his ears grew even larger and more pointed than they had been before. I could see William following him in the change and suddenly it became clear that something else was happening. I heard the screams from the sky and saw the flames lighting it.

I heard Tarvoti's voice very clearly in my own mind as she took charge. She instructed Samoda to protect me, and she had not come alone.

Suddenly I felt the wind of great wings. I was snatched up and born up into the air in Samoda's strong arms. She threw me onto the immense, luminous creature that had lit up the sky behind her.

"Hold on tight." She hollered back to me as we took to the sky.

I could not imagine in my wildest dreams how this would have felt. We were riding a dragon. The beast below me was hard. It felt as though it had armor on. I could feel the giant scales move as it moved. I was holding onto Samoda tightly with my face buried in the middle of her back. I had each arm wrapped under hers and up over her shoulders as the dragon took a turn and headed straight up. If not for Samoda I would have fallen right off and plummeted to my death.

When it finally leveled off I raised my head to see where we were and everything for miles was visible. I could see the castle that we had just been in below us, way below us. Its peaks and balconies were just barely visible. The trees that jutted up from it were like small limbs lying there unmoving. Off in the distance I could see smoke billowing into the air. I could feel the tension in the beast as it flew towards the smoke.

"Balcerak is his name." Samoda hollered to me. "He will take care of you. I have to go help my brothers and sisters."

Fear surged through me as I thought of the idea of trying to control this beast. I was not even comfortable riding a horse, and they ran relatively close to the ground in comparison.

"You don't control him. He controls himself. You just hang on.

He will keep you safe."

As we reached the first plume of smoke, Balcerak dove into it. I thought we were going to take a nose dive right into the ground, when Samoda jumped off and he turned to climb into the sky again.

"Oh, shit," I shrieked. I knew the words had escaped. How could they not have? I held onto one of the dragon's giant scales with all my might as he climbed higher and then leveled off again.

Then it happened. He looked at me. His eyes were huge and green. He turned his head back to face forward. He kind of dove a little and let out a howl followed by an enormous breath of flame. I could feel the heat from it, but yet it wasn't all that hot. It was more of an icy hot sensation. I squeezed my legs tighter around him, and I could feel his heart. It was pounding irregularly through the tough armor. I saw something as I squeezed him, an image taking form in my mind. It was like his heartbeat was some sort of strange signal enabling me to pick up another channel.

The vision was of disaster. I could see the Warriors being slaughtered. Many of them were falling and others were battling, being pushed back, farther and farther. I saw William. He was being bitten by something. The demon had wings like a giant bird and was wearing its insides on the outside. I could see the thing's bare muscles moving as it charged at William. I could see the mortal blow it was preparing to deliver against William. I knew he would be gone forever.

"Go!" I screamed feverishly to the beast, and he did. He dove into the smoke. I didn't know what I would do once I got there, but I knew I had to do something. I couldn't allow William to be killed even if it meant that I had to die. I had the distinct feeling this was all about me anyway, of course, isn't that always what a human thinks? I found my resolve even as the scale that I was clinging so tightly to came off in my hands. I knew the dragon had given me a weapon. I quickly grabbed another just to keep my balance. We reached the ground quickly and Balcerak let out a plume of fire. I jumped from the beast into the path that he had cleared for me.

So many things happened all at once that it was hard to keep track. William smelled me instantly and jumped away from the demon that was pursuing him. As he sprinted towards me the demon jumped onto him from behind. I ran as fast as I could towards him but another of the demons cut me off. This one was slowly walking towards me. he knew I wasn't fast enough to escape, so he could take his time. Finally, when he was within reach, I slashed at him as hard as I could with the dragon's scale. It sliced through him effortlessly. I smelled the raw sewage leaking out of him as he screeched in agony.

The goo that filled him spattered all over me as he fell to the ground. I could feel it sting as it hit me, but it wasn't as bad as the Quip's had been. It was a definite reminder, though.

I ran towards William, who was still fighting the demon that had jumped onto him. I landed a sharp blow to the back of the demon's neck and cut off his head. It landed right beside where William was laying. I wasn't sure who was more surprised, William or I.

There were many more pressing forward onto us. I heard the roar of Balcerak just in time to duck away from the flames that he shot at the ground. A horde of demons were coming right towards us. Balcerak lit close by to allow me back onto him, but I refused. If I were going to die, I would die right here fighting for something that I believed in. I would not cower or escape into the sky on the back of a dragon. I would stay, and I would fight with the others.

I could hear Tarvoti screaming at me in her mind: "Get the hell out of here, now!" She was absolutely furious. I ignored her words as I went forward. I swung the dragon scale as hard as I could at each of the creatures that I could get close enough to.

The other Warriors felt a renewed sense of obligation with me there. I was a mere human and was engaging these dreadful creatures and defeating them. We all fought together, and I do not think another Warrior fell.

When the battle was over I felt the urge to faint. I couldn't believe what I had done, I didn't know how I had done it. I certainly didn't want to face Tarvoti for directly disobeying what she had instructed me to do, but there I was, face to face with her.

"Balcerak showed me William. I couldn't let him…"

"I am not angry with you. You did well. You want to be one of us. I can tell. Your thoughts are loyal and true. Come, you can ride back with Samoda. The rest of us will run."

Her eyes flitted towards William. I knew she was going to talk to him on the way. It was right there inside of her thoughts. Samoda hollered at me and helped me onto the great beast Balcerak, and we were off.

As we flew towards the castle, I secretly thanked the dragon for keeping me safe and helping to keep my love safe. When we landed on a balcony on the top of the castle, Samoda bid him farewell with a short talk and then addressed me.

"You know, my dragon wouldn't give up his armor for just anyone."

She had the swagger of a professional as she walked towards me and took a seat on a bench. I could see her tense muscles relax as she kind of stretched out a little. I sat on the other end trying to give her as much room as she needed.

"Oh, I nearly forgot…" I pulled the scale out of the waist band of my dress, which was now looking much worse for wear, and continued, "Should I, here, can you return this to him for me?"

Samoda laughed. "No, you keep it for now. If he wanted it back he would have taken it." She took a more serious tone. "You are special, Kali. I know Tarvoti has tried to sway you against loving William. She has lost her love, Charlavae. I can imagine that is enough to sway anyone against love. There are times she even wishes that she had never met him to spare her the pain of him being dead. Of course, I cannot say what I would do. It hurts to even ponder the thought. What I am saying is you have been given a special grace. You are a Strega, and we need you as strong as you can be for the battle that we will fight when we return."

"I just love him, Samoda." I didn't know what else to say, because that was the simple truth.

"I have had many visions of you." She turned her face towards the ground. "I have seen you and William together. I don't know if you know this, but it *is* possible. I don't know how things will work out. I just know what my visions tell me. You could easily die. We all could. This is very serious. Our lives rest in the balance of what you choose to do. All human lives are at stake as well. You are very important to the outcome of this war, Kali."

A ruckus to my right interrupted us. Drake led the group as they came leaping onto the balcony from the stairs, with Tarvoti and William right behind him.

Samoda gently smiled at me and then rose to meet her mate. They embraced, sharing a passionate kiss that seemed endless. "Nuem has summoned all of us back to the courtyard." Tarvoti scowled. She was unhappy about so many things that I couldn't quite pick apart what was at the front of that line. Charlavae, William, the demons, and I were all a big mixed batch of disaster in her mind, and it was really starting to piss her off.

I followed them with William behind me all the way back down, six floors till we reached the entry to the courtyard. As we passed under the arched door where the red material had been draped we realized that the garden was empty with the exception of us and of Nuem. He was seated on the throne at the other end of the vast stone floor. All of the tables were still set up, laden with fruit and the steaming pitchers and bowls, but every creature, winged, small, or forest, was gone.

As soon as we were within sight Nuem waved us over to him. "Come, please sit. I have asked all of the others to go home for the evening. I think we must have some time to talk among us. We have many decisions to make. You are my Warriors. There is a battle looming on the horizon. The constant war between the Avorians and us Athenians is growing."

He paused to look down, like he was searching for a way to translate what he had to say into terms we could understand.

"I fear the spells cast by the Strega of old are quickly deteriorating. As I sit here and ponder the fact that Kali is here with us now, it is only further proof. She is at least half human, and we can all feel the evil that courses through her veins, yet a force has allowed her presence in a place that is protected."

He waved a finger to the closest pitcher of steaming Noi, and it poured itself into five goblets. I watched as the goblets floated across the floor to each of them. They took their glasses and began to sip.

My glass was right there on the edge of the stone where I had left it. I hadn't realized that I had emptied it. Before I could even reach for it, I heard a tiny giggle coming from across the arena, and then a little Serephine flew in and across the garden. She sat down beside my cup and with razor sharp teeth made a slit in the translucent skin on her wrist. She held it over the goblet until it was full to the rim, and then looked at Nuem.

"Thank you Sientria. You may retire now. If I need any more I will call on someone else."

She flitted off as Nuem excused her. I could hear her little giggle for a few moments even after I couldn't see her any more. It seemed to echo through the air.

I held the glass and wasn't at all queasy about drinking it. I was getting accustomed to this. This time the Serephine blood didn't taste quite as sweet and syrupy as Paela's had. This had a meatier taste like steak and baked potatoes with only a hint of the sweetness that I had tasted earlier.

"We have several issues at hand." Nuem started speaking as if we were in a board meeting for some corporation instead of on Atheria planning the life and death of his people. "The first and foremost issue is that the Avorian threat is coming closer to the humans. They are after you, Kali. They want her Strega powers. They want to use her to mate with one of their demons calling himself Cabe. If they can achieve that, then they could use her to decimate the humans. She would become half of Cabe, and he would become half of her. It would be that simple. They would have two demon lords, possibly three with Seline, her sister. It would also give them the powers to completely destroy the defenses of all of our protected places and have free reign inside them. Arxies, The Elder's Den, and even Atheria would no longer have any protection at all against their presence."

Nuem paused and looked directly at me to make sure that I was paying attention. We were all listening intently to every word he was saying.

"I will not do anything against you. At least not willingly," I interjected.

"I know that you would not intentionally, especially now after building the relationships that you have. You are as weak as you are strong though, and your ignorance of this only further proves your weakness." His eyes bounced around the circle of people sitting there. He knew I would not betray them intentionally.

"The next thing we must talk about is William and Kali." Everyone's eyes were on us.

"I don't think we have anything to talk about in that area. It is forbidden by law and that is that." Tarvoti's accent got thicker as she spat the words out angrily.

"It *is* against the law for humans and Warriors to mate." Nuem agreed.

Samoda looked from William to me then over to Tarvoti. I could tell she didn't want to say it, but there was something urging her.

"Is Kali purely human? I mean, she is at least partially so, but there is also the Strega, and Balcerak lent her kindness. He doesn't do that for mere humans. There is the fact that she made it here, she survived the winds of Woden, doesn't that say something about her?"

"She will die." Nuem's eyes stared at William and I, awaiting our reaction to his statement. I wasn't at all shocked, I knew I would die. I think every human knows this. The Warriors seemed to know it was part of their job, that it could happen at any time, so I couldn't understand why this was such a big deal.

"Aren't we *all* going to die?" I blurted.

That was the question I think Nuem had been waiting for. "Yes, every human will die, it was how you were made. My Warriors, however, have a different fate. When you die, your souls live on. You can and most often do have another life, another eternity waiting for you." His words softened as he continued. "They…" He motioned to the warriors with a wave of his hand. "They can live for centuries, eons, forever, if they are not extinguished by the demons. Their lives are infinite. We do not yet know what you will become, Kali. You have a human life left to determine that."

We all stopped to contemplate Nuem's words. Until William's voice broke the silence that in my mind had seemed infinite.

"I sit here allowing all of you to decide the fate and direction of the love that I have for this woman." His words surprised me. I had never heard him take this tone before. It was respectful but powerful. "Tarvoti, I understand your unwillingness to condone such a union, but your views are skewed by the loss of your love. Drake, would you not have been with the woman that you love? After two hundred years of longing for the mate that would take your heart and become one with you, would you have let her go so easily? Samoda…" William paused to smile in her direction. "Thank you for the support. Nuem, I have given everything you have asked. I have loved you enough to die for you, so is it wrong for me to feel the same about my mate? Have any one of you felt any different for your mate? I do not know why I have fallen in love with her. I do not know why you…" He paused and pointed his finger directly at Nuem. "…allowed my unbeating heart to surrender itself to her, but it has. I love her."

By the end of his speech he was standing with his arms outstretched to them, nearly pleading for permission. I adored him more now than ever. He had just professed his undying love for me, and I wanted to return it.

"So be it." Nuem stated. "I fear nothing good will come from this. I fear that the destiny that you both were made to fulfill will become skewed into something sinister. However, I have vowed to never enslave my children. You all have your own free will to make the choices that are laid before you. So if this is the path that you both wish to tread, I will not stop you."

CHAPTER EIGHT

THE RITUAL

Everyone rose to their feet. Nuem stood in front of the throne-like chair and Tarvoti reluctantly led me to one side of the rock platform. I could hear the churning of the thoughts going through her mind. She could not believe that Nuem would condone such action. She was outraged that he was allowing this to happen. William went to the other side of the stage.

I wasn't sure what to expect, and that was probably a good thing. Once I got past the anger in Tarvoti's head, I could hear the buzz. She seemed to be saying, 'Oh, Shit' over and over again. She was truly worried about what was about to transpire. The visions she was conjuring up were nothing short of horrifying. She was also worried that this would literally kill me.

Nuem raised his hand to the sky, and the wings I had seen earlier manifested behind him again. He seemed to grow to massive size, and his features changed again. He had become something else that was an even greater combination of all the creatures I had seen here earlier this evening.

I could feel him urging me, telling me, to come to him. I didn't have a choice but to obey. As I took my first step onto the stage, my bare feet seemed to find their own rhythm and began walking towards him. I saw William across the stage doing the same thing. We were walking towards one another. My feet could feel the chill of the stone on them, and if I had control of my own body I expect I'd have gotten goose bumps, but I didn't. It was as if I had been possessed by another being altogether and had no control over my own movements or reactions.

When we reached the center of the stage right in front of Nuem, we both stopped. I looked up at William, and his eyes seemed to entrance me. In them the stars were shining and the brown had turned to blue. His fangs had found their place jutting up and down along his lips. His jaw had gone from its chiseled masculine beauty to the Warrior structure that made it a little longer and slightly wider. His physique changed from a manly, muscular one to a larger, leaner, more lethal form. He was absolutely beautiful.

I felt Nuem's wings barely touch me as he wrapped them around us. The flickering lights from the garden dimmed until they were completely lost within the cocoon of black that Nuem had enveloped us. I could feel the first prickle of blood running down my back before a stinging pain set in. My hands clutched William's tightly as I fell to my knees. I could hear Nuem's voice getting louder as he spoke. Through the pain and darkness I couldn't understand any of the words he was spewing out. All I could think of was the searing pain that was being wrung from me. I had been through a lot of this lately, and this was by far the worst.

Just as I was certain I would pass out, I caught a glimpse of William. I could see into him. I could feel him surging through me. I wanted to see more. I had to find more. I kept probing, and I could feel him caressing my soul. His pain was tremendous, but not as much as mine, and he was lending me his strength. I could feel it swirling inside me. It wrapped around and embraced me until it was over, and the blood that dripped from my skin ceased being wrung from me.

As Nuem's massive wings began to release us, and the light from the flickering torches seeped around us, I fell limp to the floor. My body stung and ached just as it had before. I knew *he* could stop it with one wave of his hand. I turned my eyes upward until I found him. His light eye flashed mercy at me through the stars and moons that lay within, and his dark eye held vengeance for the pain that I had brought onto myself. I wanted to scream as he leaned toward me. He stroked my hair for a moment and whispered something that I didn't understand, and the pain was gone, completely gone. I am not sure if it was my pleading or William's that made him decide to take it from me, but whatever it was, I was thankful.

Nuem turned his back to all of us, and somehow I got the feeling that he regretted what he had just ordained. Without looking at us he poured his words into us as if they were liquor being poured down our throats. They were as harsh as badly brewed bourbon that was boiling over with poison.

"You may not regret this union soon, and yet you may. One thing is certain to me, at some time you will repent of it."

He turned back to face us, and his eyes were steel as he continued.

"Go now and do as your will commands you, but do it in the human world."

With a wave of his hand Woden was at once swirling around us. He carried us unforgivingly back to my house where we all were dropped right in the backyard in the middle of the lavender patch that Grandma had so meticulously planted.

CHAPTER NINE

THE ARRIVAL

William's arm was draped carefully over my bare shoulder. I could feel his cool touch on my warm skin. The electricity had dulled a little, but only a little. His touch still made me crave more. I could feel the stinging that the winds had etched into me once again. It wasn't as bad this time because William had shielded me. I felt stronger than I had when I had left. I could feel his soul mixed inside me. I could feel his thoughts in my mind, and I liked it. I wanted him. I wanted to consummate our unity.

Everyone else was silent as we entered the house. I didn't know exactly what they all thought, but I did know that Tarvoti was not happy, even a little bit, for us. I was saddened only momentarily by her thoughts.

William's arm was still draped around me when I grabbed his hand and headed upstairs. I was done with all of the negativity. I was ready to explore the love that William and I had.

As I closed the door behind me, I wondered if it should bother me that this had been Grandma's room. Maybe it should have, but it didn't. I was different now. I could feel the difference inside me. I had a little less consideration for right and wrong, and I didn't really care. My only care was for William. My only duty was to him. He was a part of me, and his strength coursed through my very existence now.

Before I could turn to face him, his hand wrapped around my body and pulled me close to him from behind, his free hand pulled my hair to one side, and he bent to allow his lips to find my neck. I could feel their cool touch caressing my skin, and my own heart fluttered frantically. I leaned back into him and closed my eyes to let my mind, my heart, and my soul feel everything that my senses were experiencing.

He turned me towards him and picked me up in one swift motion. It only took a moment and a few short steps until he laid me across the bed. The dress that I had worn home billowed under me. William crawled into the bed beside me. His breath was heavy as he pulled the dress apart where my cleavage spilled over the top.

"I love you, Kali. I don't have to resist you anymore."

He tore at the dress until he had pulled it completely apart to my waist. His tongue trailed from my neck to my clavicle, to stop directly over where my heart was beating.

"If I…" He paused long enough to kiss gently the skin that covered the muscle that was beating rampantly. "If I hurt you, stop me."

His words were broken among the passion, and I couldn't speak.

I just didn't want this to end.

His lips continued until I felt a slight prick under my nipple. I could feel and hear him moan in ecstasy as he tasted the sweet crimson that oozed from me.

I am not even sure when, but we had both become completely naked, and his body was against mine. I could tell he was holding his weight off me when he raised himself slightly to look at me. His eyes had changed to the blue that looked like heaven. His fangs extended from his lips. He was glorious.

I could see myself through his eyes and realized he saw me as the most beautiful creature he had ever known. I could see what looked like a tattoo peeking out around my sides, and I rolled just a little to see where it went. It ran from across my ribs to the small of my back. The tattoo was a collage of what looked like tribal markings. They were all connected with swirls that reminded me of the winds that carried us. William had the same markings in the same exact spots. His fingers trailed around them on my back until he rolled me onto my back again and continued down my body, across my stomach, and came to rest at my thighs. I could feel his fangs rake across my more tender parts until my body was pulsing with the same erotic ecstasy that was throbbing through him.

He pulled himself back up on top of me, not missing a single spot to kiss along the way until he was towering over me. I could feel him hard against my thigh and my body wanted him desperately. I reached towards him and pulled him closer to me. As he slowly pressed his weight onto me I could feel him enter me. It felt like explosions were going off throughout my body as he made love to me over and over again.

After hours of passion, we lay next to one another just staring into each other's eyes. I could feel his love within and around me.

"I love you." My words were honest and sincere. I never wanted to be without him. I could imagine the loneliness that would render on my soul.

"You will not be without me, Kali." He knew my thoughts and was answering them. "I could track you through time if I needed to." I could see his pride in his ability. "That is what I do. I will have you with me forever, whatever that takes."

I closed my eyes as he leaned over and kissed me, and I fell off to sleep from sheer exhaustion. My dreams quickly found the passion that William and I had just been entwined in. In the dream he kept asking if he was hurting me as he gently kissed me and ravished my body. He wasn't hurting me. I was stronger than he gave me credit for. Then suddenly he was gone, and I was lying in the patch of lavender that Grandma had planted.

I felt her lie down beside me. I saw her hair pulled back, and the old flannel shirt felt soft against my arm as she touched me.

"Grandma, I'm so glad you're here. I have so much to tell

you—"

"I know, my dear." She interrupted. "I know everything that is going on, dear girl. I am here to warn you, though. She is coming. She knows, and she is coming."

As her words echoed through my mind in the air around me the lavender disappeared, and I was left standing in a field of black and white. The image that surrounded me became clearer in my mind. I could see the details of the picture that was etched there before me. There was blood, and that was the only color in it. Nuns in their black and white habits and their pale skin were fallen to the ground, surrounded by a red blanket. The bodies of other innocents were either lying on the ground or falling to the ground from the slaughter. The red flowed around this black and white picture of death.

Everything in the image was wrong and out of control. I wanted to pass out just looking at it.

The horror that filled me was only stopped when I recognized the perpetrator. Her face was familiar and pained. The skin was as white as everything around it. I could see a hint of color in her hair as she turned. Her robe billowed as she swung her arm around to decapitate another innocent. I was face to face with this horror, and it was churning inside me. I could feel the pulse of it, finally, I could see through its eyes. I wanted to turn my back, but knew the vision was coming from within me, and I was held by it. It was me, I was death, I was the destroyer that was wreaking havoc on these innocent people.

I woke gasping for air with my eyes about to jut out of my head. As I sat straight up I realized that William was peacefully resting beside me. His blonde hair had fallen around his chiseled features. With his eyes shut he looked more like a statue than an angel.

I felt a pang of guilt at the thought of sentencing him to death as Nuem had implied I had done. I didn't want to believe that. I loved this man and could not bear to find him hurt by my desire.

I got up, threw on the robe that was still hanging on the back of the door, and headed downstairs. I looked back at him as I left the room and quietly shut the door. I didn't want to wake the others either. I wanted some quiet time. I needed some quiet time.

I took each step carefully even as I was certain that the creaks and moans of the old floors would have raised the dead, but when I got to the bottom and peaked into the living room I could see everyone still resting. Samoda and Drake were lying on a mattress that I didn't recognize. It was thick and black and looked like it was stuffed with feathers from the way it held them up off the floor. They had a sheet draped over them, but I could see their silhouettes entwined under it.

My eyes found Tarvoti laying on the old couch with one of Grandma's quilts over her. She looked so peaceful. The angelic look that William had didn't quite fit her but still she was peaceful looking. I could hear that her mind was resting well. It wasn't filled with the twisted burning ire that usually lay within.

I tiptoed into the kitchen and thought of how much I really wanted a cup of coffee, but decided it wasn't the best idea to head to town alone. A lot of things had happened, and honestly I was still a little spooked and didn't want to be that far away from William. Instead I opted for a glass of water and headed out the backdoor to go sit on the porch.

I took my seat in the old chair and pulled my legs up under me. I sat my glass on the rickety table next to me, and I wrapped my arms around my knees and rested my chin on them. My mind was churning. I kept wondering why Nuem had allowed William and I to mate. He had not really condoned it, but he had performed the ceremony. He had given us matching marks. Yet he seemed so disappointed with us. I wondered what he knew that we didn't. I was certain that we could handle whatever was coming and that William and I would be together until I grew old and died of natural causes. I was equally certain that the Warriors could take care of themselves and me at the same time.

"Never underestimate the power of the Avorians."

Her words startled me. I had been so lost in thought that I'd never heard her come out the door directly behind me. Samoda sat in the chair across from mine. It moaned under her weight. Her eyes were scanning the tree line.

"They are out there, and they are coming for you. My visions of you are still yet to come. It will be worse than you think, Kali. It will be more painful than anything you have endured thus far. Your strength will be put to the test. Your resolve will be strained. I can only hope that your love for William and the strength that he has granted you will be enough." There was a long pause as I contemplated her words. Then she continued. "Cabe is coming for you, and his army is strong." As she got up she looked straight into my eyes. "None of us may survive this battle."

She went back into the house. Her words had caused a chill to run down my spine and all the hairs on my arms to stand at attention. I looked about. The road was quiet. I scanned the tree line around the old house, and for a moment I was certain I saw movement. Then I realized that it was only the wind rustling the leaves in the brush. I resumed my thinking position with my chin resting on my knees. My mind mulled over the dream I'd had. I wondered what it meant, if anything. I would never do the things that I had seen. Then It struck me that it may not have been me. Maybe it had been Seline in the dream. I couldn't imagine her getting her hands that dirty though. I smiled as I thought of her even making a mud pie now. She wasn't that sort of girl anymore.

Yet if anyone could evolve it was her. She had gone from the backwoods, undereducated, stringy-haired brat that she had been to the well-educated, sophisticated, professional woman that she had become—and still I didn't know a single person that cared to be around her. I did have hope that she ran in a circle of people much like herself. One that would accept her and love her the way she was. I knew that somewhere deep inside she was good, and

I felt kind of bad that I couldn't share our heritage with her. I wondered if an adult Seline would be better prepared to handle the power than a child Seline did.

I let the thought go immediately as I noticed a sports car on the road. When it slowed down and then signaled to turn into the drive, I jumped up so quickly that I nearly fell to the ground, tripping over the robe I had on.

"Oh shit!" I exclaimed as I ran into the house. A quick glance showed me that Samoda, Drake, and Tarvoti were not in the living room where they had been. The mattress that Samoda and Drake had been lying on was gone. I ran up the stairs as quickly as my feet would carry me and into the bedroom that William and I had shared the night before. I was relieved to see him lying across the bed, still resting. I thought of waking him, but as I heard the car door slam I opted to grab a pair of jeans and a t-shirt and hurriedly throw them on. I looked back for a second before I ran back down the stairs leaving the door ajar.

When I got to the back door I saw her standing next to the car lighting a cigarette. I watched her for a moment as she took a big drag and looked around. Her eyes were bright green and her hair was still long and rusty colored just like mine.

It was Seline. She carried herself with an air of distinction, her free hand wrapped around the waist of the Chanel suit she was wearing. Even so, her pointed ivory heels looked a bit uncomfortable standing there in the dirt drive.

I stepped out the door with a smile. I was happy she was here. I couldn't help but wonder what had brought her, but it really didn't matter for a minute. She was here, and that was what was important. I loved the twin that I had shared my childhood with as much as ever.

"Seline. I can't believe you're here," I said as I walked towards her.

"Yes, well. I tried to call, but…"

There was a pause as she looked me over. I was quite certain that she was condemning the old faded jeans and t-shirt with no bra that I had thrown on.

"So, surprise. Here I am."

The smile was forced and somewhat haughty, but it was good enough for me at the moment.

"Well. Come on in."

She followed me through the doorway, after giving her cigarette a toss, and I could tell by how she looked around that she was uncomfortable. It didn't take a mind reader to know that this place was beneath her. She had grown completely unaccustomed to shabby old houses like this one.

I offered her a seat at the kitchen table, and she accepted.

"I don't have a coffee pot here. You want a glass of water? I think that's all I have to drink." I offered it politely, knowing that she would decline.

"No. I still have a cup of Starbucks in the car."

"Really, would you mind if I have a sip of it? I haven't made it in to town yet."

"It's in the console, go get it." She motioned towards the door with her hand.

"Ah, thank you." I said as I went out the door.

It only took a few minutes and I was back in the house. If I had been paying attention I would have known that William was up and on his way down the stairs, but I didn't, and when I came back in the door with the coffee in one hand there he was standing in the kitchen at the bottom of the stairs with only a pair of jeans on. He had leaned against the wall casually and was smiling courteously at Seline as they made their introductions, which I only caught the end of.

"William, Kali's..." his eyes fixed on me "...husband."

"You're married?" she shrieked. "Why didn't you tell me?"

She was excited, but I could see that the real excitement lay in William's bare chest that she couldn't take her eyes off. If I had been paying closer attention, I would have known this was all wrong. I would have remembered that I had just had a dream where I had been warned of this. I would have known that the Seline standing in front of me was more consumed with evil than she had ever been. I would have recognized that William's thoughts were in turmoil, as he struggled with his instinctive urge to destroy her and fought the Warrior inside to stay calm.

"Yes, with everything going on, you know, with Grandma. We don't talk much. I just didn't think about it."

I felt like my words were tripping over themselves. I was a terrible liar and always had been. I really wasn't lying, but it somehow felt like it. What could I tell her, certainly not the truth, not the whole truth. I couldn't bare my soul to her as I wished I could. Grandma had given me a warning against that, and I wasn't willing to forgo that warning yet.

As soon as I thought of Grandma, I thought of the dream. She had told me: 'she is coming, she is coming for you' had been the words. A chill ran over my entire body as I finally thought of it.

"Well, well," Seline said as she rose from her chair and walked towards me. "Kali Rose Marr...." She paused questioningly. "I guess it's not Marriot anymore."

She stopped in front of me with her hands resting on my arms and her eyes bouncing from William to me, wondering what his last name was. I felt panic sear through me when I realized that I didn't even know his last name.

William knew the thoughts twisting and turning in my mind. I hadn't even remembered our connection when he spoke up.

"Eaton. Our last name is Eaton."

He walked closer to me and put his arm around me to calm me. He knew that I felt as though I may explode. It worked because every nerve ending in my body was now focused on him. I knew he would protect me, and as my eyes returned to Seline I realized why I had been concerned.

The details in her face were off, and I knew the reflection, I stared at it each day in my own. Her eyes were green but not quite the right color. Her skin was rosy but just a little too much so, and there was something else that I couldn't quite put my finger on. Yet, I knew it was her. It was no masquerading Quip or trick of vision, William would have known that. He would have been able to smell it, and I was certain I would have also.

I realized his hands were behind us and had turned into the claws that I knew were part of his change. I looked up at him and could see and feel the effort he was using in suppressing the Warrior that was trying hard to emerge from inside. I could hear him whispering to my mind: "She has been tainted by Cabe. I smell him all over her." He was fighting against the Warrior urge with all of his might.

I suddenly felt like my surroundings turned to a blurry haze. I knew it was happening. At the same time Seline's face became pale as reality set in. At that moment she also knew the line had been drawn, and she would not easily accomplish what she had come here for.

I could feel my twin inside me. I could feel her soul breaking from mine. I knew that she knew everything, and this world had never really been hidden from her. She was a part of me. I had always wondered if she felt me, and at that moment I knew she did. We were as one entity being ripped apart down the middle. I knew that for either one of us to be complete we needed the other, but she knew it also. She was here to take me, to take my soul, so we could become one. She had become a powerful sorceress and had found the dark art that came from the Avorian god. She knew if she bound me that she could join us together in a way that would destroy me, but still allow her to be free of me.

Seline released her hands from my arms and turned to run. I could hear each of her footsteps down the hall as she carried herself to the front door, and I heard the slam of it behind her as she bolted out of it.

Her retreat was followed immediately by an onslaught of inhuman cries. A pack of Quip were emerging from the trees! The buzzing of the golden-skinned demons' high-pitched screams as they ran towards the house was deafening. I had to cover my ears to protect them from bleeding.

I could see through Tarvoti and William's eyes simultaneously. William had bolted out the back door that we were standing by and was slashing through the crowd of crazed monsters coming at him. Tarvoti was on the other side of the house doing the same thing. I couldn't quite place where Samoda and Drake were, but I was certain they were on the other two sides of the house fighting as well.

I caught a quick glimpse of the far tree line through William's vision, and I saw Seline. She was with a man. It was Cabe: his arm was around her, and they were walking casually behind the mass of Quips that were obviously doing their bidding. Seline looked content with herself and her demon. Cabe had gotten his hooks into her: that was the difference I had seen.

As much as I had wanted to see the sister that I knew and loved, I had seen the sister that I knew was evil, the sister that had come here to destroy me. I knew it as I saw her with Cabe. He had tasted her blood and had shown her the darkness that had been locked away. Sabine knew she was a Strega and had drawn her line in the sand against me. I knew she wanted me dead. More than anything she wanted to kill me.

Individually the Quips were easy enough for the warriors to kill, but the sheer number of them were overwhelming, and some slipped past their defense. I heard the front door open first, then the door that was behind me. I wasn't certain what to do, so I ran upstairs to my grandma's old room and shut the door behind me. I could hear them coming. I could feel them as the panic surged through me. I wouldn't go without a fight. I grabbed for the knife blade that I had used before and quickly found it in the papers that I had strung across the desk even as they pushed the door open.

There were too many. I knew I was overcome. I knew this was the end of me. There was nothing I could do. I began slashing and stabbing with the knife, putting up as much resistance as possible. I stabbed and cut at the demons, but the assault pushed me backwards towards the window.

William had felt my panic and was fighting his way towards the door. I saw the stairwell as he entered it, and I knew if I could just hang on a moment longer he would be there to save me. He dove past them, taking two steps at a time until he was at the top.

I fought with all my might, swinging harder and faster at the golden monsters. I could feel their blood which lacked the crimson appeal of my own as it gushed and sprayed on and around me. My newfound strength steeled me against the acid that splashed around the room as the fallen ones disintegrated under my blade.

I felt the window pressing against my back as they pressed me hard against it. I was thankful it was closed even as they pushed me harder and harder. I could feel it cracking under my weight. They were actually trying to push me out of it.

As the door opened on the other side of the room the glass gave way. I felt the prickle of a million tiny shards slicing through me as I fell backwards from the second floor. I heard the low screaming growl that came from William's lungs like thunder echoing behind me as I plummeted to the ground. I could see the Quips being sliced through and thrown aside as he reached the opening that had swallowed me.

Just before I hit the ground something grabbed me from above! I heard and felt my surprised scream mixing with William's as I was carried helplessly up over the battlefield and into the sky.

I struggled against whatever great beast held me in its grip, but I could not make it release me. Its strong talons were sunk deep into my arms yet oddly it didn't hurt. My mind was racing so fast with the thought of what was happening that I couldn't find the time to focus on the pain. It did, however, in some weird fashion, seem as logical as everything else that had happened to me.

A plume of fire suddenly lit up the sky, emanating from just above me. I let my eyes go upwards to see what exactly had hold of me.

The first thing I noticed were the wings, larger than anything I had ever seen. It was a dragon.

He was different from Balcerak, Samoda's beast on Atheria. The reddish-orange scales on its belly were the size of dinner plates. The colors he wore were being plucked from the plume of fire he breathed as we ascended into the darkest part of day high above the clouds. The air was cold up here and ice crystals shone like diamonds all around us. I caught a glimpse of a few shining white teeth, then he looked down towards me, and I knew immediately that I was not allowed to stare at him. He told me so without a word spoken. I looked down quickly.

The eerie feeling of being so high in the air mixed with the cold around me was making my heart palpitate. The thought that one slip of these massive talons that held me would cause my ultimate demise was enough to make me scream.

I wondered if I died now, this way, would I would find mercy with Nuem. Would he allow me that? I had not meant to do any of this. I wasn't sure if the twinge inside me was from the mere altitude or from the guilt, but whatever it was it was gone as soon as it came. I felt my body go limp one part at a time, and there was nothing I could do to fight it off.

I knew then that I had been injected with some sort of poison, and I tried to search my mind for the answers, but it just spun out of control. I lacked the understanding that would allow me to think clearly. Then darkness overtook me, everything went blank, and I faded into oblivion.

CHAPTER TEN

BETRAYAL

The floor was cold and dry. I could feel the chill had penetrated me to the bone when I woke. My bare feet felt like they would break if I tried to bend them. The jeans and t-shirt I was wearing were dusty. I could feel the dry cold through my whole body as I took a deep breath. I felt like I would choke on it. My human body had not been made for such torture as it had so recently undergone.

I opened my eyes slowly to try and see where I was. My hair had fallen over them like a tangled veil. I looked past the web of hair to see what I could, without moving.

The dungeon was dark with only a flicker of light coming from around the corner. I couldn't see the source but was certain it must have been an actual flame by how it scoured the walls, licking up and down and bouncing around.

The bars that lined the front of this cell were long and slim. They could have been made from a type of metal, but they looked more like chiseled rock that had been wound together with thickly braided ropes. The door seemed heavy enough that its weight would break the hinges right off when swung open.

The other walls were dry and dotted with sharp thorny-looking daggers of rock jutting out here and there. The ground on which I lay was just as dry. It was smoother where I had been placed, but the remainder of the room looked dangerous to walk across, especially with bare feet. The rocks followed the same patterns as the walls with sharp places here and there.

The pain in my core was intense. I was certain something was inside of me eating from the inside out. It was like hunger pains but much more powerful. I knew it was William. This was the price of our bonding, the price we had been warned of. I couldn't stand being without him. It was literally hurting me.

As I sat up I heard a low growl from outside the cell. I followed the sound with my eyes and spotted an animal that blended with the background of rocks. I had to look hard to find him. His beady little yellow eyes looked crazed and full of hatred. His wiry hair was matted around him in a tangled mess. The greenish drool that hung like slimy shoestrings from his mouth looked lethal and brought back the instant memory of the acidic goo that the Quip had turned to and burned me with after its demise.

He stepped slowly towards my cage, and at that moment I was glad of the bars. I would not have wanted to meet him face to face with no barrier between us. He was massive and strong looking. He did look a little clumsy instead of stealthy, but I didn't want to let my own preconceived ideas lead me into any worse a situation, if there was one. He was intimidating, and that was enough for me to stay put.

From a distance I could feel the vibration of something else. I knew it was powerful when even the massive dog-like creature crawled back into his spot against the wall. The vibration turned into something more. It wasn't quite thunder: it felt powerful and hungry. Then I realized it was the voice of something, a being that was busily probing inside my head. It seemed vaguely familiar.

It laughed. The cacophony of laughter coming from it sounded as if it were coming from multiple beings, and it was full of evil and hatred. The cynicism that it possessed projected itself towards me, mocking me.

I could feel the shame of indignant lust and vile contempt oozing from it as it came into view.

He was beautiful. At first I wanted to bask in the sunshine that this revelation brought to my face, then I felt the truth behind him, and I wanted to cower from it out of sheer fear. Those first opinions did not constrain the next realization, though. He looked almost exactly like Nuem, and the shock of that helped me keep a firm grasp on my soul.

"Yes, I am my brother's brother."

The laughter that once again filled the tunnels and echoed into oblivion was pulling and tearing a hole into my soul. I could tell he was mocking me now.

"You think it a trick. You think I am deluding you."

The laughter ceased and silence filled the air. Even the dog-like creature must have found another exit because he was nowhere to be seen.

The demon-filled creature that wore Nuem's appearance no longer meandered towards me. He seemed as if he disappeared and reappeared right before me. The heavy door must have obeyed his orders because it swung open right before he reached it and then slammed back against the bars with a heavy thud.

As he stood there with the light flickering around him, I recognized the differences between him and Nuem. They were the mirror image of one another. Their eyes were the same color but backwards from one another. Nuem wore his light eye on the right and this creature wore his on the left. Their hair was the same, only the part was exactly opposite.

My observations were interrupted when he spoke.

"Yes. We are mirror image, twins, as you would say. Just as you and your sister are." He paused while looking at me, or better said, through me. "Well, not exactly like you and Seline. We do not *share* a soul as you two do."

He was once again mocking me. He knew my thoughts, my fears, and my life. He would use whatever means he could to tuck me under my own shadow. He was ridiculing me with each word that he cast out.

He turned his chin upwards slightly, smiled cunningly, and continued, "It hurts doesn't it? I could ease your pain you know."

I looked at him with contempt. I didn't want anything from this monster. I wanted nothing more than to be with my William. He understood my answer quickly.

"Very well then, have it your way. The pain of separation will only get worse, and when your Warrior has fallen attempting to save you, it will consume you."

He was close to me now, speaking in almost a whisper. I cowered beneath him. I didn't want him to touch me. I knew it would tear at any good that I had inside me. This devil was devoted to either owning me or destroying me and didn't seem to really care which one it was.

"He will die, and you will belong to me, or you will die too."

I wanted to scream at him. I wanted to pull him apart with my bare hands, but I knew it was impossible. I was powerless against this creature. Yet as he turned to walk away from me I couldn't help to blurt out to him.

"I will die first."

He stopped short of the door and without even acknowledging me enough to turn toward me, he spoke strongly.

"You are human, you will not die first. You have the ultimate desire to live. You think you're strong enough, but you're a weak human. You *will* die, but not until I have used you up."

"You don't know me then."

"Oh, Kali, do not trick yourself into thinking that. I know you, I know your thoughts and your desires. I know that when you die, you will be mine. You will be my angel of destruction. You will end the war over the humans. You will destroy mankind for me." The laughter in his words taunted me.

He left without another word. The door closed behind him, and I remained in my prison.

I wondered what would become of me as the pain inside gnawed at me. William must have been feeling the same thing, I thought. I wasn't sure though. My mind pulled me back to Nuem and his own disappointment in uniting William and I. He must have known that this would happen. I thought of Samoda and her words of warning that they would come for me and they would get me. I closed my eyes with the thoughts of my dilemma. What would I do? What could I do? How would William find me? Would we survive this?

I listened as I heard the low growl of the beast that had apparently been sent back to guard me. I noticed that there was another voice, also growling with it. Now there were two of them there.

Through the darkness I opened my mind to try and allow their voices to make sense to me. I wanted to know what they were saying. I lay as still as possible and kept my eyes closed. Finally, I could make sense of the noise that vibrated from them. I could make out enough of the words to fill in the short sentences.

"Do you think they will come?" "To save their pet?"

It was followed by low growling laughter. "I think she is a mate of one of them."

"I heard Avore say that. He told Cabe she would be his soon." "Ahhh, sisters."

"When her mate dies, she will do whatever Avore wants."

Through the grunts and groans of their words, I could understand what it was that Avore had in store for me. He really thought that if he killed William, that I would do his bidding. He thought that Cabe would have me and Seline. He thought that even if I died I would do his bidding as a demon of his. I allowed the dream I had to pass through my mind. I would never do such a thing. I knew that there was nothing he could do to me that would make me do those things. I was human, but I was also a Strega, and I had mated with a Warrior. I was much stronger than he gave me credit for.

I was angry, and I couldn't lie still any longer. I rolled onto my other side to turn away from them. I didn't want to hear any more of their babble and laughter. I had to think of something. I had to get out of here before the Warriors got here.

Out of the darkness "bring her to me," rang through the walls as the first clash of thunder in a storm might sound.

The beasts slammed the door open and came for me. The bigger one went to grab me, and I pulled myself away from him. I knew there was no point in struggling. They were in control for now, so I followed him, and the other one followed me.

The hall that we walked down looked much like the cell itself. I could feel the dryness of this place around me and inside me. The beast behind me poked at me to keep me moving as we ascended the stairs. With each step I could see a little more of the terrain that awaited me.

Once we got to the top step I had realized that what I had thought I was seeing truly was real. The ground all around me was rocky. It was full of jagged rocks with big gaps between them. It looked like an alien planet or something. I had never seen anything like it. I stared into the distance, but as far as I could possibly see it was all more of the same, with the exception of the giant structure that jutted up out of the ground about 50 yards ahead of us. The big rocks that formed the walls of the building looked more like giant teeth reaching out of the ground, waiting to consume anything that would dare approach it.

I thought about running, but I knew I wasn't fast enough to outrun these beasts. I had to find a way to get away from them for a few minutes, then maybe I could make my escape. It would at least give me a head start.

I wished that I had the dragon scale that I had used on Atheria. I tried to remember what I had done with it. I couldn't recall ever giving it back, and then I thought of the knife. I had used the knife on the Quips in the bedroom. What had happened to it? I could have dropped it when I was abducted from my home. I felt my pocket nonchalantly, and it was there. I must have inadvertently stuck it there when I was taken. They had so much contempt for me that they had not bothered to search me.

I slid it out very carefully and quietly said to myself the only words that I could think of: "*Secco du lat*." I hadn't ever known what it meant, but it had been one of the few things that I had remembered Tarvoti chanting when I was in so much pain. Then I started swinging with all the fervor I could muster.

When the beasts were caught off guard they weren't all that strong! I stabbed and slashed at them until they both lay on the ground. I felt the urge momentarily to taste them, but then I realized that the goo that was flowing from them was poison. I ran into the darkness, daring the lethal-looking ground that wanted to trip and swallow me up.

I ran as far as I could then I ducked down behind a rock to catch my breath. The air here was stifling, and it didn't quite seem like there was enough of it. I hadn't run very far, actually. As I looked back at the large scary-looking building looming in the darkness, I wondered where my friends were. I wondered if they even knew I was gone, yet then I realized that they did.

I pulled myself back behind the rock and ducked as low as possible as the red dragon that had brought me here swooped low over me. I knew he was looking for me. His fire lit the sky ahead of him, but I was certain he hadn't seen me. I would have to move more slowly and carefully now. I had to be very quiet and very steady with my footing. One cut on my bare feet would be a sure way for them to track me easily.

I walked slowly, using the rocks for cover. I didn't have a clue where I was. I pondered the idea that I had been taken to some desert in another country that I didn't know about. I wished that I had been more astute with geography. That knowledge would have been beneficial at this point.

When I could no longer see the Avorian structure behind me I relaxed just a little. I walked at a steady pace until up ahead in the distance I saw something vaguely familiar. I could see the outline of a tree line. Maybe I was in luck. I picked up my pace until I was nearly jogging towards it. I was glad that I had always spent a lot of time barefooted. My feet were callused enough that I could stand the rough ground without being cut to shreds.

Once I was standing next to the tree line, I could breathe a little easier. The air was less thick and seemed clearer in my lungs. I took a big gulp of it and let it fill me completely. I hadn't had that much air since I had awakened here, and it felt refreshing. I was happy to be somewhere that I understood. I stepped into the brush-filled forest just in time. I had been concentrating so hard on reaching the trees that I hadn't realized that one of the dog creatures was chasing me and catching up to me quickly.

As soon as I stepped into the forest the creature stopped. He was pacing back and forth as though he couldn't see me, but I could see him clearly. I was no more than ten feet from him. Then I realized that he couldn't come in this space. He was near enough that the goo that was dripping from him would have spattered me if he had shaken his head, and yet he couldn't see me or touch me. I felt completely at ease with my surroundings. I still had the ache in the pit of my soul, but at least I felt safe here.

I walked deeper into the woods until I could no longer see the region outside the forest. It was lighter the farther I traveled, and I could feel the forest itself breathing with me. The lush moss that hung on everything around me brushed against me. I could feel its softness caressing the bare skin on my arms. It reminded me of the same feeling I had on Atheria. I felt safety and finally warmth in this cold barren place.

I had decided the green comfort would never end when I heard something behind me. I turned quickly to see what it was. The dainty thing that stared back at me was not what I was expecting, if I could have really been expecting anything. It was taller than me with a humanlike face. I got the distinct impression that she was a female.

Her eyes were large and slanted up dramatically and the bright green that shone in them was like giant emeralds. Her lips were a little small for her face but very pouty-looking and bright red as though they were painted with layers of gloss to make them shinier than they should have been. Her nose was small and a little pointy, but nothing in comparison to her ears which were very large and pointed straight towards the sky. They almost resembled horns. The thick cartilage looked calloused and hard on the exterior as they poked up around her long blonde locks that flowed so delicately around them. Her hair fell almost to her knees, and it seemed to be the only clothing that she had on.

"Hello," I said as though I were luring a little rabbit in to get a closer look. Then I realized that this was her world and maybe I should be scared of her. She didn't seem like she wanted to hurt me, but I had no way of knowing if when she opened her mouth if I would find giant dagger-like teeth aching to devour me or if she would offer kind words instead. My world had been turned upside down, and things were not as they appeared, not here or anywhere.

"Kali Rose Marriot, the first human mate of a Warrior." Her words were not that of a question, but a statement. She knew exactly who I was.

I shook my head yes, as though I were answering.

"You are not where you should be, human witch." The beautiful lips that were so bright red turned dark, and the ears that pointed upwards peaked. I could see her demeanor change as she began to shake her head and pace back and forth in front of me, stopping only to speak and look directly at me.

"No, you are not where you should be. Ahhh." She stopped for a moment to further study me.

I was checking her out also. Her bare skin was not the right color, it was pale green now but seemed to reflect the hues of whatever she was near. When she crossed in front of the brown tree trunk it was a brownish color; as she neared the large clump of dark green moss it took on a more greenish tint. It wasn't at all translucent, but iridescent. Her long blond hair followed her as she moved. It was straight and wound around and trailed behind her.

It looked like a beautiful dress that had been spun from gold. Her body was fit, and she seemed completely comfortable nude. She looked as though she had never worn clothes at all and had no need for them. She was muscular from head to toe, and I could see her muscles move. She stopped right in front of me.

"Vlad should not have brought you here. You cannot survive this. The odds of your continued existence at this rate are one in six hundred fifty six..." she paused, "...no, fifty seven, trillion."

Her eyes were penetrating me. I knew she was some kind of special creature, and I believed that she really knew the odds, which didn't sound very good at all. She blinked, and I realized that her blink was wrong. Her eyes blinked as if she had something in them. Each time she squeezed them shut and back open. It seemed like a strange thing to notice given she had just told me that I would probably die trying to get out of here.

"So, I'm going to die?"

"Well, your odds of that are very good. I know that Vlad brought you here, and that I have seen how that happened." She shot me a compassionate glance. "Poor girl, you have actually done quite well. The odds were definitely against you making it out of the prison Avore had made for you."

Her voice took on a very hollow sound, it sounded like it was being carried to me via old car speakers. You know, the ones with all treble and no bass.

"You do not understand any of this, do you?" Her giggle reminded me of that of the Serephine that I had met on Atheria. "It's the same old story. Avore is trying to rule you silly humans, and so is Nuem. They each want to win your soul. Those two are always battling. They always have, and they always will. At least as long as there is anything to fight over. You are an integral part of this battle. Your blood will either save or destroy all of the humans. Your choices will be the map for their destiny."

I was still not quite putting it all together when she blurted it out pretty plainly to me.

"The future of human-kind rests in the balance of your life or death."

She giggled again as if she were slightly amused at talking to a person with less than her intelligence and knowledge.

She stepped closer to me and reached out her hands towards my chest until they were resting directly over where my heart was beating feverishly. She closed her eyes and lifted her head towards the light that shone radiantly on her skin.

"You can choose your fate. You must know that death is worth more than life in some cases. In your case, it is not only eminent, but may be mandatory, if you plan on trying to save the humans." She opened her eyes and looked back down on me. "That should help you to make your decision."

She released me and stepped back.

"They already have your sister, and since your hearts beat as one, they also need you. It will complete their plan. Ironic, isn't it? They need you, and you are able but not willing, yet there she sits, willing but not able. The two of you together would make a demon that even the Warriors could not proclaim victory over. The irony is that the struggle over you humans is nothing more than a well-strategized chess game between the gods, and the odds of that changing are about as good as the odds of your survival. Come now. I will take you to my village to see my people. I know you're curious about them."

She skipped ahead of me, taking smaller steps to allow me to keep up until we topped a little hill. She seemed very happy, considering the news she had conveyed to me. I could tell that the human world held no consequence for her. She really didn't care one way or another or at least appeared not to.

Below the hill there was a large group of her species. Some were frolicking around chasing one another, and others were lying in the mossy undergrowth. She sat down in the moss and motioned for me to sit beside her.

"I feel rude that I haven't asked your name." I said as I looked at her.

"Oh, I am Kyhalu. This is my people. We are the Danbue of the middle forest. We live here. It is protected by both gods."

She watched her people playing and resting.

"Are you their queen?"

"We do not have a queen, or a king for that matter. We are all individuals. Back before your kind ever existed we lived on your earth. We traveled where we wanted and enjoyed the many treats of your land. We swam in your waters and lived in your trees. We were oracles of the gods, much like the Strega were created to be. The difference between us is that we do not conjure things to change the future, as your species can. We claim neither good or bad nor light nor dark, just truth. That is what we are, we are truth. We know the time before and the time after."

"So, you know everything that will happen? Can you tell me, I mean, can you tell me how I will get out of this mess?"

I felt a glimmer of hope as I sat next to her. She could give me the answers that I needed.

"If I tell you what is destined to happen, you will change your actions and try to prevent them. I cannot alter your will. I am bound to that law by the gods. They have given us refuge here, and we must abide by the only law that we have. I am sorry, Kali. I cannot tell you what will happen. If I do we would be banished to the outlands of Vicus and destroyed by the beasts that run amuck there. I can only tell of what has already happened and the current situation. That is all I am allowed."

She looked a little sad as she denied my request. I smiled at her to let her know that I understood. I would not want to be responsible for wiping out an entire species. As she lay back in the moss I followed her. I looked over at her, and she had her arms folded under her head and appeared relaxed but concerned. I rolled my eyes towards the sky, and as the light that shone through the trees sang me a lullaby, I drifted off to sleep.

I woke to Kyhalu gently shaking me.

Witches

"Kali, Kali, you should awaken. William is calling for you."

My eyes popped open as soon as she mentioned William's name. I could feel him. The ache inside was gone, and I knew he was close. I jumped up from where I was lying. Kyhalu grabbed my arm and turned me towards her.

"Remember, good nor bad is neither just. Truth comes from within your soul my Strega friend, and sometimes survival comes from truth, but sometimes death is the only truth left. Do not fear your future."

She pushed me away, and before my eyes could leave her she held her hand in front of her small mouth and blew onto it. The winds whipped around me, and it seemed I hadn't moved but the terrain around me was once again dark and rocky. Its sharpness caught me by surprise, and I tripped. As I was falling to the ground I felt his arms around me, cushioning me from the lethal rocks that wanted to swallow me up.

"William," I cried as I fell into his arms.

"Kali, I…" he pulled my hair out of my face to look me in the eyes, "I was worried I had lost you."

His arms were wrapped tight around me as he carried me towards an opening in the rocks. I could hear Tarvoti even before we crossed the threshold of the cave. She probed relentlessly into my mind. She wanted to know everything that had happened to me. "I guess it's good to see you again," Tarvoti said as William gently put me down in the cave.

"Yeah, you too, I guess."

I was in no mood for her haughty attitude. "You're a bit feisty, aren't you?"

I could tell her mood brightened just a little with my crankiness. Then I saw Samoda and Drake waiting in the cave.

"It is good to see you, Kali," Samoda said. "I was worried you may have been lost forever. How did he get you to this place? Did the dragon bring you all the way?"

Samoda was curious. She could have peaked into my mind at

any point and saw the whole thing detail by detail as I thought of it, but she let me tell my story.

"The dragon had poison in his talons, and I was knocked out for most of the trip," I told her. "The big dog things were my guards. I used the knife from my book to get away. And the Danbue, Kyhalu, told me a lot of stuff."

I stopped as William took me in his arms again. He pulled me to him tight and kissed me passionately right there in front of Drake, Tarvoti, and Samoda.

With the comfort of William and the other Warriors around me, I realized my exhaustion. I needed to get some rest. I didn't have to tell them anything else, they had picked it from my adrenaline soaked mind.

At the back of the cave there was a hollow carpeted with giant feathers. William pulled off his shirt, and with a wave of his arms it had become a soft red blanket. He guided me to the spot and lay down with me.

His arms wrapped around me until the rest of the world was nearly gone, everything except my own thoughts. He quickly realized that I couldn't make my mind shut off from the worries that were consuming me. His own senses could taste the dread that I would never make it out of here alive mixed with the fear of what Kyhalu had said.

He made a tiny slice in his wrist with one fang and held it to my mouth so that I couldn't help but suck as much of the sweet crimson that I could from him. It tasted intoxicating and slid down my throat like warm milk. It coated my insides and shielded them from any other thoughts. I could feel it throbbing through me until it landed in the pit of my stomach and sat there concocting a spell of utter bliss.

Yet there was a certain sadness festering inside me, the thought of William dying trying to save me. I knew I could not survive the pain of losing him. The separation that we had endured was nearly enough to pull my guts from me and leave them stretched over the distance I had traveled. If that happened I could only pray for a quick death.

"Do not worry, my love. We will get you out of this. I should have heeded the warning from Nuem."

William's words were soft as he whispered them to me. I hoped he was right. I didn't want this to end. I had never known love like this, and I didn't want to lose it. I knew it was selfish to think that when human annihilation was hanging in the balance, but I simply couldn't help it. I didn't want the human world to be hurt, but more than anything I didn't want to lose William. His arms held me as I drifted off into oblivion. I could hear his words as I fell asleep.

I don't know how long I lay there in William's arms sleeping. I was thankful it had been a dreamless rest. No demons, monsters, or even my grandma had interrupted me.

When I woke to William shaking me I could hear Tarvoti in the background of my mind. She was mulling over possible solutions to our problem, and I really wasn't all that surprised to find that one solution in her mind was just leaving me here. That plan was completely dismissed as she thought of the consequences both with William and with the demons and replaced with one that ended with my death at her hands. It would have solved some of her problems.

"How are we going to get out of here? What are we going to do?" My eyes searched his eyes as my mind searched his.

"We should get moving."

As we left the cave, I heard Samoda call to us. I could feel the uneasy tension in Tarvoti's mind growing by the moment, over something different. She could feel the dog-like creatures getting close to us. There was a pack of them, and they had found our scent.

"Come on."

Drake and Tarvoti were well ahead of us. William actually grabbed me up like I was nothing and took off. He was fast, and

I could see the others ahead of us as I bounced in his arms. I couldn't help but wonder why he would have chosen such a weak mate. The Warriors were so fast and strong, and I was somebody that he would have to carry around at the first sight of danger.

He stopped for a moment and put me down. I knew he wasn't tired, I could feel it. He knew how I felt, and he was going to give me the chance to run with them.

"I won't leave you. Just run as fast as you can. I will carry you if I must to protect you."

He ran ahead of me, but kept within sight. I ran as fast as I could without losing my balance. I really was faster than I thought I was. Of course, the adrenaline was pumping furiously through my body once again.

I could hear the howls of the creatures from a distance behind me. I couldn't understand what they were saying as I had earlier, but I could hear the desperate cries as they searched for us.

I felt like I had run forever as we reached a huge tree. I was certain I was seeing things as I looked at its branches. They looked like giant plumes of feathers. I followed William climbing into them, and I heard Drake's voice.

"What took ya so long, friend?"

The comment was followed by a little chuckle and then a small groan. Tarvoti could see them, and when Drake made the comment Samoda elbowed him in the arm. It was kind of strange to see it through her eyes, but it was still funny, and I couldn't help but giggle just a little.

The humor in the moment ceased as Tarvoti's next thought quickly passed through her mind. She was not only somewhat agitated with Samoda for scolding Drake, she actually thought, "the torture that human is putting him through, when he could have a Warrior mate like…" The thought stopped short of finishing itself but I knew she was thinking 'like me.' I couldn't believe she was jealous. That was it, pure and simple. Tarvoti was jealous of me for having a Warrior mate, when hers had died.

Witches

She didn't think of me as anything other than a thorn in her side. I wished that I couldn't see into her mind at that moment, and just as William hoisted me up higher into the tree I saw the beast circling under us, then another, then another.

"Be very quiet, don't even breath." The thought had come from my beloved William, and my not so beloved Tarvoti simultaneously. They both knew that it was unnecessary because I was so scared that I had lost all thought of air and its value. I was holding my breath so tight I couldn't even think straight.

The sky around us had lightened, and all I could see was the fluffy quills that hid us from plain sight. I was thankful that the only thing I could see was William, who was holding me tightly against him. He was standing on a thick sturdy branch with me pulled so close that my feet weren't even touching it.

Finally I had to release some of the air that was becoming suffocating inside me. His eyes were fixed on mine as I released just a little at a time, not making a sound, and sucked a little more in. It seemed like I was making gasping noises to me, but the beasts didn't hear me. Soon they left the tree and continued on their search. We stood there quietly for what seemed like hours. Only after darkness surrounded us did we climb down out of the feathery tree.

We gazed toward the lighted area in front of us. It looked like a waterfall of some strange type.

"Let's go." Samoda said as she began to walk towards it.

We all followed her carefully. As we got closer I began to see crimson boiling up here and there in the area that had looked like water. I soon realized that it was not. It was like fog rising around each little lit mass in the falls. Balls of crimson light boiled across the surface, bobbing in and out of the fog.

"What the hell is it?" I whispered.

Our eyes, one after the other, followed to Samoda and Drake, until each of us were looking between them, back and forth.

"Stop. Something is wrong," Drake spat out. His voice was tense. "What do you think it is?" Samoda responded to her mate.

"I don't know." His gaze was held by the boiling mass. "I can't see any but the red." He squinted to look farther into the area, and at the wall behind it that the crimson masses seemed to be climbing. "Samoda?"

"I can't either." She paused and stared intently into the glowing masses before turning to us. "We can't go through here. There is no way we will make it through. They are all so angry."

"Who is angry? What is this place?" I asked as I motioned to the area in front of us with the fiery balls.

"This is the Cave of Prayers. Every ball you see is a prayer. Each one can carry you to your death. They are all screaming in utter horror. Something is completely wrong."

She turned her attention to Drake, "We have to find a way back. It may be too late. The Avorians may have already…"

He nodded to show he understood what she was saying. It was pretty obvious that it was bad. I don't know what the prayers told her or what she heard exactly, but if she was worried about it, I knew I should be also. Samoda seemed like the most levelheaded being I had ever met.

They turned to run and William grabbed me up. He practically threw me over his shoulder, and in one swift motion his shirt became a device to carry me on his back. I held onto him tight as he ran with the others. He ignored my thoughts of feeling more like a pet than his mate. There was no way I would ever be his equal, let alone equal to Samoda or Tarvoti. I knew this was not the time for it, though. It was time for business, and we were headed straight into it.

I could see the tree line in the distance and before I knew it we were upon it. They all stopped, and William smoothly placed me onto the ground.

All of the Warriors had changed. As we ran I had felt William morphing into his stately Warrior physique, but I hadn't seen the others. I wondered for a moment, again, why I wasn't scared. I should be. These creatures were death in one breath. They could have killed me at any moment, any of them. Even William craved what flowed through me: humanity's evil. They all wanted to consume me, and I didn't have to read their minds to know it. It was evident in their eyes when they looked at me.

I wondered for a moment how I could have ever found Tarvoti to be the maternal, kind, compassionate, being that I used to see her as. I couldn't imagine that she was ever really kind to me. She had all along been just doing her job. She had taken on the responsibility that she had been given and nothing more. Her words interrupted my thoughts of her.

"That is it, you selfish, ungrateful little bitch. How can you have the audacity to stand there thinking that your more than what you are. You are a human. Yes, you have Strega blood running through your veins, just like me, but you, this body you live in, the mind that you think with, are nothing more than a selfish spoiled brat of a human. You have—"

I interrupted her. I wanted to claw her eyes out. I wanted to spit in her face and curse her with every word I could think of.

"I am not a bitch or a spoiled brat. You are a bitter, self-righteous old creature. I can't believe I ever admired you or thought of you in the same light as my grandmother. You are cruel and unkind, and I wish I had never met you. You are the one that's evil."

As she pulled her hand back to strike me, William appeared in front of me to take the blow. Tarvoti was strong but William was quick. Her hand struck him right in the lower part of his ribcage just as his landed across her face. They both were knocked backwards and hit the ground, and I was left standing there in near shock. William was on top of her before she could get up. He was so fast that I couldn't really see him move.

"She is mine. I will kill you if I must." He growled in a tone that shook the ground that I was standing on.

Before I had the chance to shoot a smile to Tarvoti about my small victory, William stopped me.

"She is my sister, my brethren Warrior, we are all on the same side. Do not antagonize her again."

As he turned to the darkness and ran his hand through his hair to pull it out of his face, he looked to the sky that would offer him no solace and thought, "Nuem, what have I done."

Drake's hand landed on his shoulder.

"We must press on, William. We have to find them and get our answers. It is our only hope of getting out of here."

With a consoling smile Drake shook his old friend a little bit and added, "Females, can't live with 'em, and surely wouldn't want to live without 'em."

He smiled a genuine smile of love at Samoda, and I believe she knew he was only saying that to make his friend feel better.

"I will wait here," Samoda said.

"You need to come with us. We have to find the Danbue and get some answers," Drake responded, while touching her gently on the face.

The things that went on between the two of them in their heads, I would never know, but I could only imagine the conversations they had in private.

"I met them," I said trying to break into the conversation and maybe make myself seem like I could actually be of some use to them. I knew Tarvoti was still seething with anger towards me, and I was sure that the others were experiencing some aggravation over the whole incident.

"We have all met them, except Samoda," Tarvoti spat at me.

"The smell is…" Samoda paused momentarily, "…is horrible, worse than a demon."

She looked down at the ground as Drake took her hand and led her into the forest. William and I were right behind them, and Tarvoti was behind us. We walked quietly into the forest, and as before I welcomed it. It felt safe and warm to me. I was glad we were back, actually.

In the distance I saw Kyhalu. I knew it was her. I could hear her laugh that seemed so distinct to me.

"Kyhalu!" I hollered towards her while waving my hand as high in the air as I could.

"Shhh," Drake motioned towards me. "You will scare her away."

"I know her. She is the one I met here earlier. She is my friend," I whispered back to him, in Kyhalu's defense.

The low roar of his growl told me that I should hush. So I did.

I followed them as we continued deeper into the forest. Samoda kept looking around with wild eyes. She was definitely bothered by this forest, and it was odd for me to see her this way. This seemed like the safest place in all the possible worlds to me.

Suddenly from behind I felt a light tap on my shoulder. I turned, and there she was. Her beauty was just as I had remembered from earlier. As soon as her eyes met mine, I was entranced and rendered speechless. Kyhalu's eyes stunned me long enough for her to grab me and take off through the forest with me. By the time I had my senses back to me, I was screaming for her to put me down. When we were far enough away from the others she did so. She gently placed me down and smiled down upon me.

"Kali, what your company wants is unwelcome here. We cannot be involved in this. We cannot offer them the answers that they seek. We cannot alter the future as they wish."

"We can't go through the caves, Kyhalu. We have to get back, to save the humans. You must understand."

"I understand much. They can go through the caves, it is you that cannot. You will die, and they are trying to protect you. Remember, good or bad is neither just. Truth comes from the soul." Her voice trailed off as she disappeared back into the forest and

I heard the Warriors coming. "Hey, I'm over here."

"Why did you not stay with us?" William's anger was evident in his tone.

"Kyhalu took me. She wanted to talk to me alone."

"Where is she?" Drake took a defensive stance as he spoke.

"She is gone again. You all keep scaring her off."

I knew I had to tell them, so I began speaking as honestly as I could. "I know you all can get through the caves without me. You are trying to protect me. Which is sweet and all," I smiled towards William in a half-hearted way, "but I think you all should leave me here and go on without me. I will be safe here in the forest. After you save the humans and figure out a way, you can come back and get me."

"We will do no such thing." William proclaimed instantly. "It is out of the question." He was shaking his head while speaking.

"We can't do it." Tarvoti said quietly. "We can't do it. You have to help us. It is the only way. We have to have you to save the humans, Kali. Your blood is going to be what saves you all. Only your blood will do it. Trust me, if my duty didn't depend on your life, I would have already killed you myself."

As William began to say something in my defense, she cut him off.

"Really, it's the truth. If you hadn't fallen in love with her you would want to do the same thing." As she looked around at the others, she added, "You all would."

I wasn't surprised by her words because I knew they were lying there under the surface anyway.

I looked to William to find the answers that I sought. He may have been the only one here that I really trusted at this point. In his eyes I saw a million things. I saw his love for me along with the pain that he would suffer from losing me. I also saw that he would not leave me here, even if it meant certain death. I was left with no choice but to go.

"Okay, I hope it's the right thing."

"You cannot know what we know. The Danbue are truth seekers. They are truth, but they are not likely to reason out the *right* thing to do. They only know what will happen based on the current situation, but situations change. They are bound by their oath to not interfere. They do know other exits from this place, though, and they have to tell us. It is our destiny to save the human race and yours to help us do so. Let's go find them. We need their help."

Drake's words were hypnotic, and I understood very clearly what I had to attempt to do. He had made it clear that it was necessary for me to help them.

Drake led us, followed by Samoda. William placed me in front of him for safekeeping, and Tarvoti followed him. We plunged on through the forest until we were standing on the same hill that Kyhalu and I had sat on earlier, overlooking the family of Danbue below.

Tarvoti projected her thoughts towards me: "Stay here with William. If they get you, they will use you as leverage against us. We will go down and capture the ones we can."

It was that simple. William and I hunkered down in the grass with him on top of me hiding me, pushing me into the mossy earth as he watched them descend on the clan below.

Samoda was still apprehensive about being here. I could see it in her actions. She seemed more human to me here than I had ever seen her. She looked like she was following Drake's lead. Her instincts relied on his. She was literally borrowing his strength to get through this.

I was able to peek out around William's massive stature and watch them as they snuck up on the Danbue. Then they struck. I could see Kyhalu fall to her knees as many of the others took shelter in the forest around them. Most of them disappeared into the trees and with my human sight, I lost complete track of them. They could have been part of the forest hovering above us, and I could not have seen them. I could only see four of the Danbuc who had been caught, on their knees below. Drake managed Kyhalu and one other that appeared to be a male. Samoda and Tarvoti each had one captive.

They prodded them back towards us. We rose and William took the one that Samoda had. Samoda walked with me at the back of the line as we began our trek back through the forest. It took a while. With the Danbue as hostages we moved slowly as they tried to escape at every opportunity. Occasionally, Kyhalu looked back at me with tears in her eyes. I knew she thought that I had set her up. I wished that she had known, and then I realized that she did know. She knew all, and if that truly was the case, then she was crying over something else, our futures maybe.

The Warriors kept their warrior form the whole trip. They looked dangerous and lethal. Their long claws were more gentle with the Danbue than it looked like they wanted to be and not a single fang was satiated.

When we reached the edge of the forest we all stopped. The Danbue had begun struggling fiercely once the edge was within sight. They could not deny the Warriors' strength though. They could not escape.

"Look at that, Fark. You can lead us through the caves, or you can show us the way you enter the human world. The choice is yours." Drake spat the words at the Danbue creature that he obviously knew as Fark.

"I cannot show you the way, Drake. You know this, old friend," Fark responded.

"I will drag you all through the caves then. You know I will do it. If the demons don't get us on the way, we will all surely die in the caves. It will all be in vain. You will sentence your family to that fate?"

"I will not, you are the one in control of this Drake. Not I."

Fark's voice was smaller than he was. I could tell that he was trying to manipulate Drake with his words. He had reminded him that they were old friends, and that he was the one actually passing sentence on us all.

"How 'bout I throw you out there and see how long it takes for the demons to find you? Your family will surely show us then, or they will suffer the same fate."

The wry smile on Drake's face made me cringe. I would not want to be on the receiving end of his vengeance. He was showing a side that I had not seen. All signs of kindness hid from his face, and he was very serious with Fark.

"How about this...?"

Drake moved just right and Fark was able to slip away from him. He took to the trees immediately and was out of sight. In a swift movement Drake was right behind him. After a moment of rustling above us they landed back to the ground. Drake was on top of Fark with a single claw on his right hand buried in the Danbue's arm. I could see it hooked inside his skin and trying to poke through the other side.

"Fark, I do not wish to kill you. We must escape this hell, though. You *will* show us the way."

"Stop!" Kyhalu yelled as she threw her hands into the air. William had her in his grasp as she pulled from him. "I will show you. I cannot suffer this anymore."

She looked at me and mouthed the word, remember. "It is on the other side of our village. I will show you."

Her words trailed off, and I knew by her voice that it was no trick. She had given up. She did not want to see Fark suffer any further. I thought for a moment that she was in love with him. Then I quickly realized that he was her brother.

"Fark, my brother, we will not die in their war. Come, help me lead them."

She bent to help him up. William and Drake were still standing close enough to grab either of them if they tried to escape as she helped him to his feet. She ran her finger over the claw wound, and I watched it disappear as though it had never been. In its place a small red marking formed. It was a symbol of some sort, but I didn't understand what.

We walked back across the forest the same way we had come until we reached the valley where their village sat quietly. Nobody had returned yet. I figured they could probably communicate with one another mentally, or that the others were following in the trees waiting till just the right moment to spring their family from our party of kidnappers.

Once again, I was proven wrong when we reached an opening in a steep hill. It reminded me of a cave that I had been in when I was young. It was large on the outside, and as soon as we got a few feet inside the walls narrowed into small passageways just wide enough for one of us at a time to fit through.

Fark was first, followed by Drake, then in line, Kyhalu, Samoda, the other two Danbue, Tarvoti, me, and then William, bringing up the rear. Nobody spoke as we shimmied our way through the narrow passage. We reached a spot where the walls fell away. I couldn't tell exactly how spacious the chamber was exactly, but I could tell it was very large. The ceiling was about twenty feet high and could see small rays of light peeking in through cracks in the ceiling.

"Is this it?" Drake's voice echoed around the room.

"Not hardly, my friend. You would not want to enter the human world here. You would be torn apart in the Complentorium of the Universe." He chuckled as he answered.

"The what?" Drake responded confused.

"You Warriors believe you know everything. You forget if not for us you wouldn't even know who you are. You do not know of the Complentorium because it is not of your realms. It is of ours. It is the truth of life and of death. It is the all-knowing answer to everything. It is the doom of everything that is not Danbue. I could send you there and rid myself of the problems you are causing us." He chuckled again. "I do believe I will enjoy watching the destruction you are bringing to the human world, though. You know not what you do." He chuckled again.

"You have shown me nothing. I found my own way on Vicus. Your species reek of disgust." I was slightly surprised to hear Samoda speak. She seemed more like herself now than she had in the forest. For some reason, that I didn't know, she had a problem with the Danbue, a big problem.

"Yes, you are right, Samoda. You are foreign to me. I do not see you in the past or the future, and yes, sometimes the truth is very unappealing."

My eyes had adjusted to the dim darkness, and I could see Fark's eyes staring hard at her. He didn't know her or anything about her. I started wondering about her part in this ordeal. She was special in her world, and it showed in everything she did, said, and, from what I knew of her, thought.

"Shall we continue?" Fark once again took the lead. We went into another corridor off to the right and continued down it. As we neared another opening I could hear the trickle of water. I relied heavily on William's sight. My human vision kept coming and going in the darkened places. With his mind in mine I could see everything, though, and we held a complete conversation unknown to any of the others. I believe even Tarvoti was so preoccupied that she wasn't listening.

"Are you okay?"

"Yes. I'm just worried about what will happen."

"It will be okay. I will protect you."

"The way it sounds, I may have to step up and do some protecting. I just wish I knew what to do."

"You will know when it's time, and I will be there to help you. I won't let anything happen to you. I love you."

"I love you too, William."

The mental conversation went in a different direction when he began thinking of our time together making love. As I tried hard to stay focused on the task at hand, which was just to maneuver through this cave, I found it hard to concentrate with his thoughts focused on ravishing my naked body.

Finally we got to another large room with a shallow stream running through it. The moss that hung from the ceiling was lit by the light that was falling in sheets in one spot at the other end of the room. It was a larger opening in the top of the cave. The air was thick and smelled damp, but fresh and kind of like rain. The musky scent was comforting. I could feel the earth around me, and I knew

I was home. I was back to the earth that I had been swiped from by a big evil dragon. Since then my world had changed. I kept finding more and more out there that I had no idea of. I knew for certain that life as I knew it would never be the same.

CHAPTER ELEVEN

CHASING EVIL

The Warriors climbed through the opening in the ceiling and then William pulled me up through it. The trees that jutted up around us were massive. I could tell that we were on a mountainside. The trees that I could see below us were just as tall as the ones right around us, but as I looked down I could see their tops. The air was crisp and smelled sweet.

The Danbue followed us, and as the light touched their skin it became lighter and even more iridescent. They completely changed right before my eyes. They seemed lighter in weight than they had. Wings spread from their backs, and in an instant I watched them fly into the daylight and disappear into the treetops, and then they were gone. They were finding their seat for the ensuing battle between good and evil, the battle that would define the outcome of the human race.

"We should go straight to the cave. We have much preparation to do," Tarvoti said as she took off ahead of us.

I could feel the tension in William's mind. The sweetness that this world held for me held something more disdainful to them. They could smell it. It was arid and raw in their throats, and I could feel William aching to run wild, chase it down, and consume it. He was extraordinary in his reserve, though.

He ran slowly with me, while the others went ahead of us. I

knew he wanted to go with them, but waited for me patiently as I ran at my human pace. I caught a glimpse now and then of Samoda and Drake in the trees. They were chasing one another back and forth through their tops.

Finally we reached a spot where a tree had fallen. The limbs were intertwined around one another. I could see a hole in them as William guided me in front of him into it. He followed me until we were through them and standing in a small opening in the side of the mountain. The hole at the bottom was not very big and looked like a narrow tunnel. I crawled through first and emerged in a huge room where the Warriors had already gathered.

The ceiling of this place spiraled up. The cave itself looked as ornate as the furnishings. At the very center of the spiral in the ceiling was a small opening. It was like a pinwheel.

The rooms that led off from the main chamber looked lavish. Each one had a picture hung above it. I knew immediately which one was Tarvoti's, because of the portrait of her and her beloved hanging above the door. I couldn't help but feel some sympathy for her. The picture reminded me of a youthful Warrior. This was a time before the lines in her face had become present and her calloused heart had petrified from the pain of love.

The trickle of water off to the far side of the room sounded soothing. As I looked closer I realized it was like a miniature waterfall that flowed into a stone basin that was big enough to use as a tub. I was certain that was the purpose of it. The steam that rose from it let me know that it was even heated by some force of nature. I could imagine soaking in it and allowing my troubles to disappear into the fog that surrounded it.

In the center of the room was a large wood table. It had carvings decorating its sides. There were chairs all the way around it. Each chair was also intricately carved, and they appeared to be only a little different in their detail. Several had been moved away from the table, and that is where the Warriors were gathered. While I was caught up in my enjoyment of this sacred place, they were looking down at the centerpiece that was placed in the middle of this huge wooden slab.

I recognized the smell of the sage and lavender that Tarvoti already had burning. They were arranged around a large white pillar candle in the center. I looked closer and could see the sprigs of the sage sparking as they caught hold of the fire. Around that was a gathering of things that I didn't completely recognize. There were different leaves and branches. I thought I saw some red berries in the mix, which I'm certain would have been holly. One of the few things I had read in the book was that it was a good repellant for evil spirits.

Tarvoti's eyes caught mine. She didn't have to speak to tell me what to do. I knew she wanted me over there. I walked towards the table trying to keep my eyes on her, but the flame kept calling to me also. It was as though it was screaming at me to pay attention to it. I managed to make it to the table without falling prey to the voices in the fire. Tarvoti kept my mind busy with instructions.

"Keep your mind on me until I tell you. Don't look at the fire. Try to be brave, for this. I have to add your blood to the mix. Don't look. Just look at me. After I make a small slit in your wrist over the fire, you can look at it. You will see many things. Try to remember everything that you see. I will also try to look in your mind and remember what I can, but it may try to block me from your mind. It will be okay, Kali. You have to do this. It is the beginning of your part in this battle, and from here there is no turning back. You will be bound to finishing, good or bad."

I held my hand across the table to her, and I could feel William probing into my mind. He had taken his place across the table behind Tarvoti to watch. I looked into his eyes as she made the slit in my wrist. It felt deep, and I could feel the blood ooze out of it. I didn't want to look, but I could hear Tarvoti screaming into my mind "Now, look into the fire. Remember all you can."

I felt the fire pull me into it as soon as my eyes caught the first glimpse of the flame. It was hot, and I instantly started to sweat all over. It was so hot that the sweat dried as quickly as it formed. I could feel the blisters forming on my bare skin. I wanted to fall away from it, but it was too late. I was consumed by it. It had me in its grasp and wasn't about to let go.

I saw something outside the fire and began to drag myself towards it. I couldn't tell exactly what it was, but one thing was certain, it was on the other side of the fire and I had to get there or be burnt alive.

The closer I got to the edge of the flames I realized what I was pulling myself towards, and I had the utter desire to return to the flames. They were beings, tall creatures who wore their muscles on the outside, much like the creatures that I had fought on Atheria. I could see the wads of tendons that resembled balls of spaghetti working between the slits in their muscles as they moved. The mouths in their long faces spewed profanity of the worst kind. They each had swords that they were slashing with. They were attacking a crowd of people, and I had to look closer to see who they were. They were innocent, I could tell by their screams and pleading for mercy. They only wanted their lives. As they fell one by one, I could see the balls of fire rising from their ashes and disappearing into the air.

As I turned to hide my eyes from the massacre, I saw another scene to my right. I saw Quips much like the ones that I had seen before, only these were much more defined. They were stronger and faster. Their legs had matured into thick well-formed limbs. Their arms touted their muscular power with every stride they took. They were like grown-up versions of what I had known. They were chasing something. I began to run towards the scene to see what it was all about. They went over a small hill, and as I topped it I could clearly see the whole thing.

The whole valley was on fire. Between the plumes of smoke rising I could see the battle. The Quips had herded angels into the valley. They looked like the Danbue only smaller. There were thousands of them being slaughtered. Some by swords, some by the lethal venom of demon talons, and some by teeth that were tearing them limb from limb.

I had to hide my eyes. I couldn't see anymore. I couldn't hear the screams of the victims. I couldn't feel the intense pain of their demise any longer.

I looked for the flames in which I had come and could not find them. In their place was a woman. She wore a cloak that was hooded, and I could only see her back, yet I knew she was a woman. I could feel her pulse beating within my own. I could smell her. The pain that she was fighting she projected as anger. I saw her swing and swing again. The sword that she wielded was magnificent. The blade was shiny, and through the blood I could see the shimmering jewels that decorated the hilt. With every innocent that she destroyed her pain lessened for only a moment, but that moment was worth it to her.

I ran towards her. I had to stop her before she could do any more damage. The closer I got the stronger I could feel her. When I was within reach of her she turned swiftly towards me, drawing her sword against my neck at the same time.

Her hysterical laugh made me shiver. Her face was splattered with the blood of her victims, but she was still recognizable. It was Seline. I wanted to cry. As sadness overtook me, I remembered her at the farm. Obviously a lot had happened since then. Now she was an even more powerful dark creature with little left of the sister that I had known.

Between her laughter I was able to make sense of what she was saying: "You will die by my sword, sister."

Her words were calloused and cold as she spat them out. I wanted to ask her why. That was the burning question in my mind. How could she have become so evil?

I fell to my knees as she pushed slowly into my skin with the shiny metal. The pain became bearable as I realized that she too had fallen. She struggled to get up and finally staggered to her feet.

In a distance I could hear the voice of William, screaming in agony.

"Bring her back now."

Over and over his words mixed with his anger as he catapulted his way through the fire to rescue me.

I felt his presence in this world as soon as he arrived. I found a small glimmer of hope of survival. I knew, at the moment, my strength was no match against Seline's, so I fell away from her blade and rolled in hope that maybe I could be quick enough to escape the blow that I knew she was preparing to strike.

I heard her laughter again as I got to my feet to run. She landed two blows across my back cutting an X into my flesh. I fell forward onto my face. I tried to move, but somehow I could not. I could still see everything going on around me. I saw Seline turn to flee from me, just as I realized it wasn't me she was running from, it was William. As she limped into the distance I could see the blood running down the back of the cape that had the same X- shape carved into it as my back now bore.

William was loping towards me faster than any of the creatures here could possibly move. The smoke was still everywhere as he scooped me up from the ground and turned to run back towards the flames.

I felt a mixed reality swirling around me as I faded from existence. I could see myself leaving my body. I could feel my limp corpse that William was clinging to for dear life as he swam relentlessly through the flames. They were fighting him as he went through. I could feel them lick my face, but it no longer burned me. I could not find a way to get back into the lifeless body that William held. I clung to him, trying to keep up as we were spat out of the flames and thrown back into the cave.

I watched as he laid my body on the table and ripped the remaining clothing away. Tarvoti moved the concocted centerpiece of candle, herbs and branches above my head. She ran to her room and quickly returned with a wrap of some type. She held out a cloak that was as ancient as the world. It had been hand spun by the angels, I could tell, with material as fine as the air around it. It was black, with red accents on the collar and edges of it. On the back, in the center, was a large sword that ran from the top to the bottom. The hilt was very ornate and resembled a Celtic design of some type. The sword was woven in with golden thread. It shone brightly, contrasting against the black fabric, as she started chanting above me.

"Hey, I'm here," I said. When nobody responded I said it again. Then I began screaming it, still with no response from anyone. How could William not hear me? My soul was bound to his and his to mine. How could he not know I was right here, or at least my soul was. I watched Tarvoti trying to revive the human body that had been badly slashed. She rolled me over and could see the X that had been sliced into my back. She instantly began to touch the open wounds. They began closing. I didn't know what to do. I went to the body and tried to move it. I tried to lie in it. I couldn't make it do anything.

All of a sudden I could see something else in the room. I watched it out of the corner of my eye as I tried to keep an eye on what Tarvoti was doing as well. The indistinct figure turned into something. I could make sense of the wings first. They were massive, and as they spread I could see him. I could see the shape of the God that had allowed me my mate. I could see the god that could have stopped all of this in an instant and yet he stood there just watching.

I went towards him.

"Why? Why won't you do something?" I screamed the words at him as I begged him. "Make it stop, make it all stop."

I motioned to William, who was doubled over in pain at his loss. I knew he was being ripped apart from the inside out.

Nuem's eyes found mine, and I could see the remorse as he spoke. I could see them water with the blood of the blameless people that had been victimized.

"I cannot stop this. I should not even be here, but you are

special to me. I wanted to usher you home myself. I should have sent Cimeran, but I wanted to see you one last time. I wanted to try to explain this to you."

Nuem's words were as confusing as ever. I could not make sense of what he was saying exactly.

"I won't go. I am not leaving him." I motioned to William, who was full of pain and becoming more consumed with anger every second. "I will not go."

I emphasized the last sentence.

"You must go, Kali. You do not have a choice. You do not belong here any longer. You—"

I cut him off. I had all I could take. My whole soul was literally being poured into my words. Since that was all that seemed to be left of me, what difference would it make now?

"Do not tell me what I am or where I belong. You did this. You could stop it all and make amends for it all. You could put me back in my body and allow me to live on. You could allow me to stop this madness, or you could stop it yourself. You could turn me into one of them and make me whole again."

His arms were outstretched towards me.

"I could do those things, but I am bound by the rules that I myself set as law. I will not lower myself to the cheating, lying, depravation that Avore has sunken to. They would have won your soul. If you live, they will win you. You are not as strong as you think yourself to be. You are a very weak child. I have allowed too much already. I should have let nature have its way many times before. I am your God, but I cannot be your savior now."

"Please, I beg of you. Do not do this to your devoted Warrior. William does not deserve this."

I found that even in spirit only, I was on my knees in front of Nuem, begging for my life back. At the time I had no way to know if it was purely out of devotion for my mate or was one last selfish attempt at life as a human. Whatever it was that pulled the words from me, Nuem conceded to allow me to live.

Witches

My attention was drawn back to my body as my back began to sting with the same pain I'd felt when Seline had sliced through it with the sword. Samoda was standing next to me with her eyes closed. Her head was turned upward. Her hand was resting on my back. The wounds were opening up and blood began to pour from them. I could feel it all. It was stinging and burning just as it had before. I could see Seline standing behind me as she had when she had delivered the blows.

Nuem was fading in front of me. His words diminished as well. "Your love will torment her, but only your death will kill her."

His form returned to a mere shadow, and I felt like I was being pulled back into my body. I went willingly. I wanted to be back, I didn't care about the pain anymore. I just wanted to be back in William's arms.

Suddenly, my eyes opened. I had reclaimed my body and rolled over. I opened my eyes to see the swirling ceiling above me. The pain was excruciating, but I was alive.

"Hurry. Bring me the knife." I heard Tarvoti scream.

"No…" was all I could whisper. I didn't know what she had in mind, but I didn't want to be cut again. Then my voice was silenced as she raised the blade above me and quickly slashed downwards across my chest.

Oh, shit, not again. Why did I have to go through this? What was the purpose of this? I let myself go again as my head began to spin with the swirls in the ceiling.

"*Secco du lat. Stregga secrato de losio.*" I heard the words swirling with my mind and the ceiling.

"Elements of the God Nuem, we need you once again. All of human-kind's existence is at risk."

I opened my eyes to see the ceiling begin to crack and open above me. I wanted to jump from the table and run. I looked to my left, and I could see Drake holding William to keep him from running to me. I turned my eyes towards Tarvoti and Samoda who were holding me on the table, one on either side of me. I barely struggled against their power and gave up quickly. I could no longer feel the stinging in my back, only in my chest. I could feel the blood trickling down my ribs. The robe that encased me was becoming as blood-soaked as my tattered clothes had been.

I smelled them before I could see them. First it was the smell of rain mixing with the dust of the earth. Then I could feel the air around me stirring, and the heat of flames wavering around. The combination smelled powerful, and I was sure that I shouldn't look. I got the feeling that I wasn't worthy to see what was swirling above me. I kept my eyes closed.

"Spirits of the elements, we offer blood of a Strega for your help. We need to heal this human and make her whole again. We need for you to touch her and heal her."

"What is it that Nuem says of this?" The great rain poured out fluidly as she spoke.

"Nuem has sent us to this earth. We are his Warriors and are tasked with keeping mankind safe. We are paying our toll in her blood for you to do so. Rain, please wash her clean of her pain. Fire, we ask that you sear her wounds closed to keep them from bringing her death. Earth, give her shelter while she heals. Woden, dear wind, bring her back to us when it is time."

Tarvoti's pleas were convincing. The spirits began swirling ferociously around me. They were swiping at me and licking the blood from my body. I could feel them all the way around me as they picked me up from the table and pulled me into them. They carried me to darkness where I rested. My eyes opened and closed, and I was at peace. I had no pain and no agony. I neither felt William nor didn't feel him. I just was. It was as though I was suspended in time. I relished the feeling, which was at times even giddy with the feeling of liberation and freedom while trapped in the hole that had been designed just for me by the elements.

The elements I had taken for granted my entire life. I had cursed at them on rainy days and admired them as the sun set on my face, but all in all, I had taken them with a grain of salt, and now they had protected me and become my savior in a world that I had never imagined existed.

I continued to think while lying there, but funnily enough, not about really anything serious. I felt as though I were being reset onto a track that I might come to regret. I couldn't find a reality that seemed likely and real in this darkness. I was happy but not too much so, I was sad, but not overly so. It was like the middle ground. I imagined for a while that I was average. I imagined that none of this had happened, and I was merely lying in bed awaiting morning to come, but mostly I just lay there in the darkness and thought of things that had no real meaning.

CHAPTER TWELVE

THE AWAKENING

When Woden came for me my life once again changed, which neither surprised nor shocked me. I was becoming accustomed to the frequent adventure of not knowing what would be coming next. He whipped the ground around me until it was not even a shell encasing me. I pushed my hand through it and was blinded by the light of the dusk on the outside.

I didn't have to rise from the ground by myself. Woden pulled me into him and carried me off. I could feel his wind whipping around me, and I felt different. I could feel the stinging of it on my skin, but it was not as intense as it had been before. Maybe, like everything else, I was getting used to having my skin sandblasted. I could feel everything, as a matter-of-fact. I could smell everything also. I could smell the ground that had mixed with my own scent to create a cocktail that seemed smooth and sweet.

I'm not sure how, but I had been awakened fully clothed. I had on jeans, a t-shirt, and boots. The t-shirt fit snug against me, and I felt rested and energetic. I felt strong.

Woden spun me until he released me onto the ground. I was at the foot of the stage on Atheria, on my feet, right in front of Nuem.

The woman standing behind him had a serene look. I had not seen her species when I was here before. Her face was porcelain and she glowed against the lightness of this place. Her eyes caught me in a trap, and I couldn't release them. Her smile allowed me to break free. Her familiarity was kind, and I smiled back at her. She was like an angel that a month ago I would have envisioned.

"You have asked much of me, Kali. I have given you what I can. I require only that you use this responsibility for the good of mankind." Nuem's tone was serious, and he didn't make any small talk. "You only get a moment with her."

He motioned to the lady standing behind him and then stood up and walked away from us.

As soon as she opened her mouth to speak I realized who she was. "Kali, you have done well to stay alive, my child."

"Grandma." I fell into her arms and held onto her tightly as tears poured down my cheeks.

"Now, now, do not cry. You will be fine."

Her words soothed me, but I knew she was just quelling my fear. She did not know if I would be fine or not. She had no way of knowing.

"You are an angel yourself, my dear girl. You must focus on saving the humans. I know you will. You must destroy your sister to do that."

Her words became darker, just as her appearance did. The glow that she had worn turned to a black hue all around her. I could feel the anger pulsating from her as she continued, and it caught me off guard.

"Do not fear me, child. Your sister is the one who slaughtered me—her and the demon, Cabe. Seline lured me out, and he attacked me. My mortal body was tormented and slain, but my soul is that of a Strega Oracle. I lived well, and Nuem has offered me grace in this realm. Remember, your blood is the key."

I looked at her in awe. I didn't want to leave her, but I knew I had to.

"I love you, Grandma. I will do my best."

Those are the words that I left her with as Nuem walked

towards us to signal that our time was over.

"You must go now. You must go join your brethren and your mate and fight this battle in the war against the evil taking over the humans. You are many things now. You always have been and always will be a Strega. You are still very much human, but I have given you what you will need to fight this battle. Be warned, however, if you do not use this wisely, my wrath will be your death, and it will be final. You will have no more chances as a human, or in my realm."

He looked at me intently before finishing.

"It may not be enough. Now go, before it is too late."

With his words Woden grabbed me up and spun me back to earth.

When I reached my destination I felt the familiar scent of my mate. William was not weeping, instead he was angry and strong.

He was not mourning his loss instead he was slashing at the wind god trying to free me from his bonds. His razor sharp claws cut through the wind until Woden finally released me into his care.

William whisked me up in his arms before my feet could even touch the ground and ran. I could feel the trees slicing through the bare skin on my arms like little knives with the speed of his gait. Finally he stopped.

He knelt to the ground and gently placed me onto it. He pulled the hair back from my face and stroked my cheek delicately. I could feel his claw rake against my skin. I didn't feel the blood that should have trickled down my cheek. Instead I felt the electricity that I had once felt with his touch. I was different though. I could feel the change in my own heart that wasn't beating as fast as it should have been.

I pulled myself off the ground and stood. I wasn't taller. William still towered over me at his height of about seven feet. His hair fell long and straight as I looked into his eyes and drank in his beauty.

Just as I was about to speak I heard a familiar sound. I could smell the rancid odor that the words carried with them. I felt my body tense up, and I spun around to face it.

There was nothing there. I began to follow the sound of the voice that was calling to me: "My queen, you are here for us, we knew you would come."

The smell was stronger with every step, and I continued to follow it until I was running through the woods. The ground beneath my feet seemed like a springboard. Each foot landed perfectly on it and catapulted me into the next step which again seemed to land perfectly. I had been in decent shape, but this was new. I could have never kept this pace on Vicus where William had to carry me on his back to keep from losing me. I liked this.

Just as I had grown comfortable with the pace that I was keeping, I was upon the Quip. We were face to face. The anger that I had for this creature was only matched by the curiosity that it inspired. I stood there close enough to touch it.

I could smell the rawness of his skin. The golden eyes that stared into mine spoke volumes to me.

"My queen," I heard it say. I wanted to know why it thought I was his queen. I wanted to know what it was and why. What part did they have in this event, other than just being pawns in the battle for the humans' lives?

"Why do you call me your queen?" I demanded from it.

As its mouth opened, the squeal that came from it was deafening. My hands instinctively went to cover my ears, but I could hear its voice again. It was high pitched and reminded me of trying to listen to a radio station that was being crossed with another one and full of static. I listened carefully.

"Cabe told us of your coming. He told us that you will lead us into victory. With you as our goddess we can feast on the blood of our enemies."

I wanted to ask it why the hell they were trying to kill me then, but I knew that they really weren't. It had just seemed that way. This creature was really just an innocent pawn. It was a montage of creatures that was truly dumber than it looked.

As I looked more closely, I could see the tears in the corners of his eyes. He was sad and distraught. He was merely in search of a queen to rule him. What he didn't realize was that it was all a lie. The demon had given them life through nothing more than death. He and his brothers had been born of pure evil.

I reached my hand out to actually touch him, knowing the pain it could cause me. As I touched the Quip I knew exactly what he was, but before I could go any further William was upon him. He began to rip the Quip apart, and even before he was done Tarvoti, Drake and Samoda were all there, ripping this beast apart as well.

I understood its nature. The Quip that I had watched them devour was a combination of human, vampire, some sort of bird creature, the crazy giant rabid-like dog-like thing, and a Strega. The blood of the Strega had come directly from Tarvoti, from a battle they had been in last year in Romania, and from my own sister, Seline. That was all I had gotten from the Quip.

William's touch interrupted my thoughts. His hand was cool on my arm as he grabbed me and pulled me towards him in an embrace. I completely understood what Drake and Samoda had. I had it with William, and even though I hadn't partaken in the consumption of the Quip, I could feel the erotic tension pulling at me through William.

I wasn't as big, as fast, or as strong as the Warriors were, but I was more so than before my near death experience. I had awakened transformed and was now Strega and human, with a slight mix of Warrior, all at once. I was ready to pursue Seline and Cabe. I was ready to join the Warriors on their mission. I was ready to give the Danbue what they were waiting, in the treetops, to see.

I followed them as we ran back to Elder's Den to prepare. The battle would be great. The battle would be merciless. Most of all, the battle would be dangerous, and with the mix of things I had become I was cautiously ready to pursue it. I felt nearly invincible, even though I knew I wasn't. I also knew one wrong turn and I could end up in a non-existent state. Nuem had warned me of it. I took his warning to heart. I only hoped that my human weakness wouldn't result in my demise. It was a chance I had no choice in taking though. This was my destiny, and I had to fulfill it, one way or another.

CHAPTER THIRTEEN

SISTER DEAR

I had few memories of the childhood that was intended to be forgotten. Among them was the fact that Kali was always the golden child, while I was left to fend for myself. They wonder how I had gotten this way. I say, how could I not have?

I remember more about my birth than anyone should. I knew I should have died, and I did for a moment. It was the longest moment of my life. I didn't want to come back here, but I was touched by the God that knew all, the God that sentenced me to life as a second to my twin, which may as well as been a long torturous death. With his touch my infant body and soul regained breath, but something was missing. Something had always been missing, and I learned to live without it. I adapted. I bet now he wishes he would have let nature take its course and allowed me to perish as I was designed to do.

As I stretch out now on the couch, healing from the wounds on my back, in my grand Chicago home, I can't help but think of the misery that got me here. I had been born to a mother that never loved me, a father that I never knew, grandparents that I had been nothing more than a burden to, and a sister that always outshined me. That was over now. I would never look back. Once I had rid myself of my twin, Kali, I would finally be free from all of that.

That misery was gone now. I couldn't help but smile as I

thought of Cabe. He is my world. I have never known love like that. He has given me everything I have always wanted, passion and power. He loved me like I was the only woman on earth. He allowed me the power to finally take control over myself. I was no longer Kali's sister, the bad seed. I was Seline, a beautiful woman with the power to rule the world. He had promised a queen's throne and a kingdom to rule over.

I thought of the day we met. He was glorious. As I left the office that day my life changed. The scene was fresh in my mind.

The street was busy as I turned after locking the heavy door. He brushed me, a little hard, and my purse fell to the ground. As I bent to the cold concrete to pick it up, he handed it to me.

When his eyes grazed mine I couldn't pull away. The depth of them had me held, and instantly I wanted to fall into his arms.

"Excuse me, miss." His voice ruptured something inside me as it penetrated.

The touch of his skin was electrical. The slight touch was enough to thrill me.

As he turned away from me I wanted to grab him to keep him from going. He must have felt it. He turned back to me quickly.

"Would you like to go out?"

I couldn't believe it, he had asked me out. I could feel the smile from the inside out as I responded with a simple "yes."

We climbed into his beautiful silver Saab. We headed straight towards the clubs and after a night of dancing and drinking we went back to my house. He was the party. Every girl in every bar wanted to be with him, and he denied them all. He may be the first person that had ever held me in the ways that he held me. He touched my soul.

I slid my hand down my body as I thought of the first night with him, right here on this very couch. I closed my eyes to imagine it was him touching me. Just thinking of the cool touch of his hands on my breasts, followed by the wet chill of his tongue flickering across my body was enough to make me moan.

Witches

Kali thought she knew me. Little did she know of how bad I had really become. I didn't care anymore. I could conjure nearly anything from inside myself. I may be the most powerful witch left on the planet. I knew I shared this with my sister, but if only I could destroy her, I would be the only one left. I would never have to live in her shadow again.

Cabe will see to it that it happens. Right now he was out in search of her. He wanted her destroyed as bad as I did. He understood my pain. He too had the same pain left scarred on his heart.

I opened my eyes and let my thoughts wander to another place. I thought of the look on her face when he tears her apart just as he had Grandma. That was the first time I had seen him as he really was. I have to admit that it scared me at first, but then I realized how beautiful he was. I tasted her blood off his body and knew that he was the most powerful man I would ever know. He was the one I had been waiting for.

I hadn't even heard the door open when I felt him on top of me. His hands roamed my body. His icy touch sizzled through my thighs as he pulled at my panties to remove them. I could feel the tension building in the pit of my existence. He pulled at me until I was flushed with the heat of passion. I felt his teeth easily slide through my skin as I felt myself release. I could feel my body fall limp for a moment. Everything inside me gave way to him. He owned me, but it was only because I allowed him to. I had given myself to him without reservation. He could do with me what he liked.

"Has she been destroyed?" I asked.

His teeth sank deep into my neck before he could answer and then he didn't have to. I could see the answer right there. I could see that she had escaped with her newfound friends. He could also see the whole scene in my mind and when he released me. I could feel the slap of his hand, hard across my face. It felt hard and stung my cheek for only a moment. He had given me the power to feel a little less deeply. He had given me the power to mask much pain.

"You tried to kill her yourself?"

As I pulled my head back up to face him I answered brazenly. "Yes, I did. I have a huge gash in my back in the form of an X now."

I stood up and pulled what was left of my shirt off. I turned my back towards him so he could see the mark that I had unknowingly etched into my own back.

"I want her gone so desperately that I thought maybe I could just do it myself."

His hand found the side of my face that he had just slapped. I knew it was red and would probably turn purple from the blow, but now he gently stroked it, and his anger had subsided.

"You know you cannot. We must find a way to put a spell on her. Or at last resort, get her to join us."

The last part would have been Cabe's choice. He wanted her just like he wanted me. He wanted to taste her blood on a regular basis. He wanted to be able to love us both and keep us for himself. He was certain that if he could have us both that he could rule not only the human world, but heaven and hell also. He would be the Supreme Being. I knew that, and I didn't care. I still wanted him. I wanted his love all to myself, and I would not allow that to happen. He would have me alone or neither of us. I would see to that.

"No," I blurted out, determined to reject that idea. "She must die. You will always have me, but never will she lie with you. Never will you drink from her."

With a blink he was gone. I knew he would come back. He wanted what I had. I only had to figure out a way to get rid of Kali before he figured out a way to lure her into his keep. If he had her, he wouldn't need me. As long as he only has me, he will need me, and I will be the one in control. I really don't care if he destroys this world. I don't care if he and I are the only ones left in it, as long as he doesn't have her. This world has nothing for me and never really had. I didn't give a shit what happened to it or the people in it.

I went to my bedroom and pulled a pair of panties out of my drawer and slid them on. The silk felt good against my smooth skin. I grabbed a pink silk button up shirt and a pair of white skinny jeans. I topped the ensemble off with a pair of stiletto pink strappy shoes that matched the shirt, and I was out the door.

Tonight I wouldn't worry about my sister who had already annoyed me enough for one day. I would be carefree and drink until I couldn't drink anymore. I would then come home to an empty house and enjoy my dreams of her demise. I would wake another day tomorrow to plot my revenge on her once again. Maybe, just maybe, tomorrow would be the day that I got my life back, the day that she dies.

CHAPTER FOURTEEN

SEARCH AND DESTROY

Drake and William were both thinking simultaneously about Cabe, they were ready to destroy him. They were enjoying the idea of ridding him of his soul, in their minds they were torturing him by taking turns sucking the life out of him until he was completely gone, vanished from this world, or any world for that matter.

Tarvoti had her mind on another world. She was still stuck on Vicus. Her mind was still thinking of the Danbue, and all they had said. She couldn't help but conjure up everything I had thought about what Kyhalu had said as well. She was wondering if I would ultimately die. She really didn't care if I did, but she hated to see William go through that. It was hard for her to reconcile with. She was a Warrior first. Nothing stood in the way of that. She had a job to do, and she would do it or she would die trying. She had been that way in her life, and she was that way in her death. Her unbeating heart had a loyalty that could not be rivaled. Her pain and anger drilled a hole into me that I could not fill with vengeance. I had already forgiven her for what had happened on Vicus at the edge of the Danbue forest.

In the safety of the Elder's Den we were all much less tense. Here we were secure and seemed to be bonding together as a group.

Samoda came through the tunnel carrying a bag with her. "Here, Kali. I know you must be starving." She looked around the room at the others and with a smile added, "I can't believe I was the only one who thought of it."

"Well you are the newest of us. You probably still think more like them than any of us would," Drake said and slapped her playfully on the butt as she walked by him.

"Yeah, well, I didn't know what you liked, so I just grabbed a few things."

"Anything is fine," I said graciously as I opened the bag and pulled the bag of chips out. I put them on the table, then pulled out the packaged ham and cheese sandwich and the raspberry zingers. "Thank you for thinking of me, Samoda."

"You're welcome. I wanted to go for a run anyway."

As I eagerly unwrapped the sandwich and started eating they began talking. We had to devise a plan to search out Cabe and my sister. We had to ensnare them and destroy them. That was the only thing left to do. The Quips would be the easy part. They were only strong in numbers. However, I did get a chill when I thought of the excursion I had made and how they had evolved. We had to get to them before they became stronger, or we would have a whole new threat to deal with.

"I think they are in Chicago. That is where Seline lives and where she would be most comfortable," I interjected as I stuffed some of the zinger in my mouth.

"Do you really think they would stay around there?" Samoda asked.

"Well, I'm trying to think of what I would do. I know the one place I would go would be home, if I could. If Cabe sought out Seline, and we know he did, then he found her in Chicago. I would bet they are still there. She has something he needs, her blood. He is feeding off of her, so he will stay close to her. That also may be where is making his army of Quips as well."

"Kali, that actually makes sense. I think that is where we should go," Drake responded.

Samoda disappeared into the room she and Drake had rested

in and reappeared carrying a small stack of clothes and a pair of boots.

"Here, you should go change. I think these will fit. If not, William can alter them. We need to get moving."

William and I went to our room, and I quickly disrobed and began redressing. There was no need for Williams to make changes. Everything fit to perfection. The jeans had a few tears in the knees and were jeweled on the hip pockets. The t-shirt was a deep purple color and swirled with lighter shades in the center of the front. The boots were strappy and flat soled. Silver buckles hooked each strap on the outside of each one and they were very comfortable as though they were made for my feet. When we emerged from the room everyone else was ready. Samoda and Tarvoti had both changed and were wearing very similar outfits as the one I was wearing.

"We are ready." Drake said and looked at each of us before crawling back through the tunnel that took us into the setting sun outside the Elder's Den.

I was surprised at how fast I could really run now. I followed William who kept track of me mentally. He knew exactly where I was, and I him. The others were ahead of us, but not by far. I ran through the forest leaping over fallen trees and over smaller creeks with the agility of a Warrior. My beating heart felt like it could explode at any minute as the adrenaline pumped through me. I wouldn't stop though. I would keep up with them the very best I could. I would prove my worth to them.

Finally I came to the top of a cliff where they had all stopped, waiting on me. Woden swirled violently in front of us. I bent with my hands on my knees to catch my breath.

"Let's do this."

I wasn't sure who had said it, and it didn't really matter. One by one we jumped into the wind and allowed him to carry us into our destiny.

This trip was as different as all the others had been. I no

longer felt the stinging of sandblasted skin. I didn't keep my eyes squeezed shut. I opened them and watched. I could see the colors churning, an array of rainbows mixed with the deepest colors of sunset. I saw them turn from brightness into a monochrome blackness and back again.

I could smell the earth mixed with the turbulence and knew this was the father of the elements. I knew by the smell that this element could rule the others. He could blow out fire or he could nurture it. He could blow rain away from her target and pull her into another realm

I could taste the vengeance that this god could inflict as well as the sweet relief he could whisper to anyone he chose. Woden was powerful in the greatest degree and demanded respect. He would settle for nothing less.

As he released us from his grasp I realized that we were not where I thought we would be. We were not in the greater Chicago area but had been dropped directly into the yard of the house that I had been taken from not so long ago, the house where the Quips had pushed me from the window and where I had been abducted by the giant red dragon that was the epitome of evil. It seemed like a lifetime ago even though it had only been days before.

In the dusk the house looked, or more so felt, different to me. The aura around it was that of doom and despair. The looming threat of evil felt ever-present. Samoda was the first one to react.

"Take this." She tossed the knife that she had pulled from the sheath hooked to the side of her pants. I caught it as if I had been catching knives my whole life. I flipped it and had it in my hand so I would be ready if anything that jumped out at me.

As we passed through the door that had been left wide open on the side of the house, I thought of several things. One was that I couldn't depend on the Warriors to keep me safe. I was in this as much as them, maybe more. It was me that Cabe was after, and I would have to use what I had been given and protect myself at all costs. Two, the words that Kyhalu had told me: the irony that the struggle for humanity was nothing more than a well strategized chess game between the gods and that the odds of that changing were about as good as the odds of my survival. Finally, we hadn't gone where I had expected. We were dropped where Nuem had summoned Woden to drop us, where he deemed us needed, and three, why were we needed here?

I could sense that the Warriors had all quietly gone in different directions while I was left in the kitchen. I looked around in the darkness and began to slightly relax when I could see nothing around me. There was no noise other than the hushed footsteps of the group I was with. I wondered again why we would be here if our enemies weren't. It just didn't make any sense to me.

At the same moment that the Warriors came running back through the kitchen and out the door I heard it. I followed. As we ran towards the tree line I could hear the screams of the monsters that we called Quips. As the screams quelled I could hear the scrambling of them in the thick underbrush. In the darkness I couldn't see the Warriors in front of me. The only one that I could pinpoint for certain was William, and of course he was quite far from me chasing some that had gone in a different direction.

I stopped to get my bearings. I turned and could see the small field that I had just run through with the silhouette of the house behind it. I stalked carefully and quietly, sniffing the air. One was very close to me. I could feel him. I could hear him thinking. I could smell him. I followed the scent that my mind was leading me to.

If I had been an actual full-fledged Warrior, I would not have hesitated. I would have dove into him and consumed him without remorse or contemplation. But I wasn't. I was still part human, and the curiosity that I felt toward this creature still had me wondering.

"What the hell are you and why—"

I was taken back before I could even finish the sentence. This one *smiled* at me. He smiled a wry smile that looked taunting. It didn't look sad or just misguided, it looked mean and nasty. At the end of the smile I saw the teeth.

"Holy shit. You're a vampire?"

"Yes, among many other things. You cannot win this fight, Kali."

There was no hissing sound in his voice. He was as different as I was now. They were all as different as I was. They were beginning to evolve. They were getting smarter and most likely much stronger.

Fear alone drove me as I leaped towards the monster, landing a blow right across his neck with the knife Samoda had given me. He fell to the ground without another word. No scream came from him. He was dead and beginning to disintegrate before I could even step over him to search out another one.

We combed the woods the rest of the night. At one point I found myself on the Cater's farm and killed one that was preparing to attack another of their cows.

I had taken the time to look in the window. I saw Mr. Cater napping in an old recliner with his shotgun right beside him, leaned up against a table. I was certain Mrs. Cater was in bed. He had stayed up to listen for and kill whatever had been killing off his cows.

As I looked in his window, I couldn't help be disgusted by the feeling that came over me. I somehow thought for a short second that he looked tasty. I thought of how his blood would feel sliding down my parched throat. I couldn't believe the thought and dismissed it as a part of being human and chasing down vampire Quips in the middle of the night in rural Missouri. I was one of the good guys, and would never do anything like that, even if I wanted to.

At daybreak we met back in the field around the old house. The Warriors didn't seem to be even the least bit tired from their night of destroying demons.

"They are getting stronger by the moment. We have to keep moving," Samoda insisted. "Kali, are you up for it, or do you need to rest for the day? We can come back for you tonight. I think we will have better luck searching for them at night. They are hunkered down for the day now. These are not day walkers."

It made sense to me. They had morphed into vampire-like creatures and would probably be more nocturnal.

"Yeah. I should probably get some rest. Do we have any way of knowing how many there are?"

"Not really," Samoda answered. "There could be thousands." She paused and looked to the other Warriors. "I think we should have all of the Warriors in the states get involved. I think we should call them in. The Quips could be multiplying on their own now. They may have an alternate agenda of their own. They may be making their own army of resistance."

They all nodded their heads in agreement.

"Kali, you rest. You will need it, and we will contact the other clans here today. Tonight we will come back for you, and we will head towards Chicago to find Cabe and Seline."

William locked his lips to mine and before I could say goodbye they were gone, and I was left standing alone in the field. I walked into the house, closed and locked the doors, and went up the stairs. I thought of how far I had come in the few short days since I had been summoned here by the death of my grandma.

I thought of everything in this world that I knew, and I wondered about all the things that I didn't. I knew that I would never again be surprised by anything. This world had nothing new to offer me. The books I had read on monsters, love, and anything otherworldly would have nothing to offer me. I had now known this world. I had experienced it, or I could at the very least imagine it.

CHAPTER FIFTEEN

SAMODA

It came as no surprise to Drake that sometimes I just wanted to be by myself. He had no doubt about my love for him, and there were duties as an Elder that I could not, or would not, deny. My first allegiance was to Nuem and the tasks before me. That was why Nuem had picked me in the first place. I didn't carry the bitterness that Tarvoti did towards humans, but I did carry the same lethal hatred of evil. That was non-negotiable in my world. That was my job, to know and destroy evil that didn't belong here on earth.

I was comfortable in the treetops. They whispered to me and gave me a solace that I couldn't find elsewhere. So I headed straight up. The closer I was to the sky the easier life was for me. I could only wish that my Balcerak would come down and swoop me up to another realm where the earth looked like nothing more than a grid of one-inch sections and then disappear beneath me.

I understood Tarvoti and her dilemma with Kali. I myself have been wondering if we should have just killed her when we first found her. There are some things that humans just shouldn't be a part of, and I think that we have found one of those things. Now she is so important to the outcome of this war that we cannot lose her.

I think back to Kyan as I stand here in the top of the tallest sycamore tree I have ever seen. I cling to its tiny top branch with one hand and look out as far as the eye can see. I think of when I literally knocked her head off with my bare hands. I had thought I could save her. I believed that she was good in the most basic of ways. I can't help but compare Kali to her. I can't help but wonder if her demise is the answer to the whole problem.

I recalled the girl with two faces from my dreams. They were as different as night and day. I wasn't aware that they were even two separate people. I had seen her as one being in my dreams.

Yet there were two of them. I couldn't help but wonder if I had been right all along, and my visions were not reliable at all. Maybe, they were just some sort of minor physic ability that was left over from a human world that no longer existed for me. I had known about William and Kali though. I had known that they were destined to be together. They were meant for one another even if that meant they would both perish. I knew that somehow, from the visions.

I felt Drake's intrusion, an unspoken "Do not doubt yourself, my lady." The seriousness of his thought was followed immediately by the playful challenge to a race. I catapulted myself out of the tree and landed gracefully on a lower branch in another tree. The chase was on. I could feel him right behind me. We both hit the ground running. We ran through the trees so quickly that before we even realized it we had run a hundred miles and were on the outskirts of St. Louis.

The city held a particular tempting scent. I craved it. It was broad daylight, and I wanted to search out whatever it was that I smelled. The rotting stench of evil was prevalent here. It was pulling at the Warrior inside of me, and she was begging for release. I couldn't help but give her some reign as I ran.

Drake and I kept to the outskirts of the city so as not to be spotted by humans. We ran so fast that they probably wouldn't have seen us anyway. I thought back to a time when I was vulnerable and weak, my human years. There was more than one occasion that I had thought I had seen something in the woods and could find nothing there upon closer inspection. I had marked it up to imagination. Now I knew that it could have just as easily been Tarvoti or one of the other Warriors running, chasing down some evil that didn't belong.

When we got to the river we turned and made our way back up it, running the whole way. The arid feeling this evil left in my throat convinced me that we had to find it. The closer we got to it, the stronger my senses became. I could sense this evil easily. It was strong and ripe with utter disgust.

We got to the epicenter of the decaying scent that had drawn us here, at the foot of an old abandoned building right by the river. The worn exterior had more than a few bricks missing. The windows were mostly broken or boarded up entirely. The large "For Sale" banner was weathered and torn, and the bright yellow on it had faded to a dirty cream color.

The smell coming from the building was atrocious. It coated my throat with hunger. My mouth became even more parched as Drake and I each took a door, his in the front and mine in the back. We could move simultaneously knowing exactly where the other one was and seeing exactly what the other saw.

Once inside, the room was empty. I could feel them all around us though. I knew they were here. This wouldn't be all of them, but it was a colony. They had gathered here and were infecting all of the humans that they could. The ones that would see their lifestyle as a means to advance their own social well-being were being targeted. They were feeding off the homeless and helpless in this area. They had set up shop here and were now resting in their peaceful little abode of sewage and discontent. They had definitely become smarter, but not smart enough, because here we were to destroy them.

I met Drake in the center hallway of the first floor. We had decided to attack them together instead of separately. They were in the basement and on the fourth floor. I could tell that was where their unholy minds were obliviously resting. We headed to the basement first.

There was no need for a sneak attack. They would all know soon enough that we were here, so we bolted down the stairs in one leap. When I landed right beside Drake they were already stirring towards us. Their screams alerted the others, and as we dove into the mass of them they began to fall, one by one, until they had all hit the old dirty concrete floor of the basement.

The ones from above had joined them, and they also met their demise. Once the whole lot of them were destroyed, Drake and I ascended the stairs. I made a final scan of the building. There were none left here. We left as calmly as we had entered.

As soon as we got back to the trees we hit the treetops, making our way back to Kali and the old house. I put the other clans of Warriors on alert in the country with only a thought, and they would join us in our decimation of these Quip vampire creatures. Our focus was once again on Cabe and Seline, who was the other face of the girl I had seen in my visions. War had been waged from our side, and they would pay dearly.

Drake and I made a leap from one tree towards another one when Woden scooped us up. He spun us above the treetops and so far up into the sky that the ground looked just as I had wished for earlier.

As a Warrior, I knew that Nuem favored us above all his creatures; although, I had never heard his voice on this earth. As we soared above the clouds I could hear his whisper in my ear, "Come to me, my child."

Drake and I landed on Atheria in the middle of the courtyard in Nuem's castle. He was waiting for us at his throne. His massive body was standing, and his wings were outstretched.

"Come, my children, I have something to tell you." We hastily walked to our god.

"There is only one ordained Elder left on earth. You know that is Tarvoti. It is, however, time for you to join her completely, Samoda. It is time for you to become an Elder of the Warriors.

You have always been destined for this and have already assumed the duties."

His eyes were focused on me, and I was gracious in my acceptance. I knew to kneel before him. I could feel his wings encapsulate me, forming the cocoon that I knew would be followed by pain. I also knew I could tolerate it. It would be another step on the rung of the ladder of hierarchy within his soldiery. I knew it would be what put me on top of that ladder and would allow me to lead my brethren completely.

As I knelt there in darkness, I could feel my body begin to sting. I could feel the markings being etched into it. The pain seared through me as he marked me an Elder. When it was over I felt new again. I was stronger than before, both physically and mentally.

When Nuem released me I could see everything as it truly was. I looked at Drake and knew that he wasn't chosen, not yet, but it was possible he would in the future join me as an Elder. I could also see that he didn't mind. I was now his leader as well as his mate. He had always given consideration to my every thought, and now he was obligated to follow my orders.

Before I even got a chance to look at my newly formed markings, Nuem's voice rang out, and his hands reached for the sky.

"The danger is becoming greater. Cabe is there. He is with her.

You must go now."

Woden spun us back to the ground, and we landed by the old house. When we got up to Kali's room, she was not there. William was lying in a heap on the floor. His body was bleeding all over. He had gashes in his bared bicep on the right side. His face had a long slice running from over his left eyebrow all the way down to his chin on the right side. It crossed his lips at a diagonal, leaving them lying open and blood oozing from them. His left leg had nearly been severed, and the meat in it was exposed to the outside.

"Go after them," he whispered as Drake knelt beside him.

"Go help Kali. He will kill her."

"Stay here with him Drake, I will go after them. You help William." I had about enough of this shit. One thing was for certain: Cabe and Seline were pissing off the wrong Warrior. I was officially an Elder now, and one thing you shouldn't do is to mangle one of my Warriors. On Atheria they may belong to Nuem, but here in this world, there was only two Elders left, and that was Tarvoti and I.

She was by my side in an instant, and we took to the place that we were both most comfortable: the treetops, following the scent that Cabe had left for us.

Tarvoti was actually overjoyed for possibly the first time I had ever seen. She had been once again given a companion. I wouldn't comfort her in the ways that Charlavae had, but nonetheless I was bonded with her now more deeply than ever. She had always known it would likely come to this and silently thanked Nuem for the gift. I have to admit that I understood more of why she was so adamantly against William and Kali's union. I felt instinctively more protective now over the Warriors. I felt like it was my duty to protect them. If even one fell it seemed that it might hurt me also, maybe not as devastatingly as losing a mate, but still I knew I would feel the pain of it.

We both knew what we were running towards and why. We really weren't running to save Kali. We were running to save humanity. We were running to save what Nuem held dear: their race. We were running to seek our revenge for William. We knew he wasn't dead. We knew he would be all right in time, but we knew the demons could not go unpunished for their deed. They must pay for the life that they thought they took.

CHAPTER SIXTEEN

CHICAGO

When my eyes opened there wasn't much difference in the darkness that had encompassed them when shut and the darkness that surrounded me with them open. I closed my eyes again and listened. There was nothing, it was as if I were entombed deep beneath the earth, far enough down that nothing could penetrate it. I was instantly reminded of the crypt I had been in while I healed. This was far different. There I had felt cozy and comfortable. This one had a sinister feel to it.

I began to let my own thoughts sort things out. What I knew for certain was that Cabe had taken me. He had gotten me with the help of my sister. She had wanted to kill me right there, but Cabe wouldn't allow it. He was happier taking his ripe anger out on my Warrior. I didn't think that William was dead, but with the gnawing pain in my stomach, I wasn't certain.

I was even more pissed at Seline. I wanted to kill her dead. How could she have done that to me? I wondered, really, how she could be this way. I had always loved her. Grandma had always loved her, yet she had aided Cabe in killing her.

Even as ill-natured as Seline was, I couldn't imagine why she has done all of this. Could she really just be evil? Was she born into it? Was this like a predestined thing that she couldn't be cured from? I had begun to think so. She was born as a bad seed, and that was just how it was. She and I had shared the same DNA since conception. I could not understand how she had become so evil.

I would have to seek her out and possibly the Warriors would save me the turmoil of having to kill her myself. Maybe Tarvoti would find the kindness in her soul to do it for me. Then again, I wanted her dead, and I could feel the rich pleasure of her death growing inside me. I would and could do it myself.

So the next question was where I was and why was I alone? I tried hard to remember anything that had put me here. I couldn't, the last thing I remembered was Seline and Cabe. Her face was lit up with his arm around her. Again I fought against the anger at her to try and see more clearly into the situation. The creatures, I had gotten a glimpse of them as they grabbed me. I continued to try to make sense of it all, but it just wasn't completely coming together. I knew they had beaten William when he tried to stop them. There was just too many of them, and they had slashed at him until he couldn't even move off the ground. I recalled seeing his bloody body, ripped and torn, lying there as they dragged me out of the house.

I let go of that thought and focused on how to free myself from this place. I could stand, and I had no shackles holding me there. I was free in this dark place. I stood and began to feel my way along the walls. I tried to imagine where a handle would be as I felt my way along in search of one. Surely there was an entrance, and that would mean that there is an exit.

I would escape this place and find the Warriors. I knew they would be looking for me, and even if the others were to give up, William would not abandon the search. He was a tracker and would find me if I didn't find my own way out. I could just wait for them if I had to. However, I would try on my own while I waited. I felt the fire of the power that I had burning inside me. Nuem had given me renewed strength, and I wasn't about to lie down and die now. I would let that fire fuel me.

After feeling my way around the walls and finding three

corners I was beginning to wonder if the escape route was above me. Just as I thought it, I found the handle. It was cooler than the stone walls and much smoother. I grabbed it with both hands for fear that I would lose it in the darkness. Trying to be very quiet, I pulled at it gently and then pushed. It moved a little when I pushed, so I pushed a little harder.

I had opened the door enough to stick my head out and still there was no light. I would have thought that my eyes would adjust to the darkness, but they had not. This was the kind of darkness that even a cat could not see in. I again felt my way around the wall of the room, going to my left. I came to an opening and wondered if it were the only one.

My mind conjured all sorts of things. I didn't know if I were entering a maze of tunnels that would gradually take me farther down until I were lost to everything forever, or if I would be confronted by creatures with gnashing teeth and gooey green slobber hanging from their mouths. I knew that I had to trudge farther along, though. I took a deep breath and proceeded carefully. I had to allow my senses to get me out of here. I was part Warrior now, and I was willing to confront whatever demons I came across, just like in the woods. I would kill what I had to.

I kept my left hand on the wall and stretched my right one out to see if I could feel the other side and sure enough, I could. The walls felt damp and cold, but the stone was rough. I tried to feel the shape of the stones. It wasn't smooth like concrete. I thought maybe it was block. As I traced a block I was certain that it was bigger than a brick, maybe more like a cinder block. It gave me a little more comfort to know that I had found something slightly familiar.

I was moving very slowly when my foot found the first step. If I had been barefooted I would have stubbed my toe against it, but I wasn't, I was completely clothed just as I had been when I was taken.

When I had awakened at home, I realized that it was nearing

dusk. I had known it was about time for the Warriors to return. I had gotten up and gotten completely ready. I went to the outhouse and did my duty there and came back into the house. I was waiting on William when I heard what I thought was him. I should have known that it was not. I could feel the pulsing of his mind throbbing through mine somewhere in the house. I didn't realize that it was Cabe and Seline until I heard the Quip's scream. As I began to run down the stairs to make my escape, I was caught.

When my eyes had found Cabe, he nearly tore the Quip apart to get to me. He didn't want it to kill me. I could remember him telling it that. He had screamed at it furiously, "Put her down now." His voice had echoed like thunder right there in the house.

William had gotten there quickly, but not quickly enough. I saw the Quips tearing at him as he tried to get to me. I remember Cabe telling them, "Him, you can have. Enjoy feasting on his soul. Do not let him leave here alive." Yet I knew he was alive. I could feel it in the pit of my soul. He was hurt, but he was alive, which meant that he would find me.

I found the next step and then another. I was ascending, which my mind found great pleasure in. The stairs wound around, and at the top of them I could see light coming from around a door which seemed to illuminate the room. I felt the jubilation of one small victory.

I found myself practically running towards the door and nearly tripped over a fallen piece of wood that was lying on the floor. The door was high enough up that it was just out of my reach and probably used to have stairs that went to it, but they were long gone. I looked around the room. I was certain it was an old foundation that had been either closed off or had a dilapidated house set on top of it. Either way, I was escaping; I was getting out of here. I found the wood that I had tripped over and pulled it with all my strength to position it under the door. I pushed it up to lean it against the wall. Even with the strength that was pulsing through me it was heavy, but I was this close and nothing was going to stop me now.

I got it up and stabilized against the wall and tested it by standing on the bottom and kind of bouncing just a little. It was creaky, and I wasn't sure that it would hold my weight at the top, but it would be a short fall if it didn't, and after all, I had already endured having the skin ripped from my body, how bad could it really hurt to fall a few feet? I got to the end of the wood quickly and pushed the door. It opened with little effort.

The outside came rushing in as the door gave way, and who would have thought that Chicago had so many trees? I wasn't sure how I knew, but I knew I was there, in Chicago. I stepped out to survey my surroundings and let my eyes adjust to the brightness of the light. The old house that stood behind me was a dilapidated old building, just as it had been in my thoughts. It towered high above me, but had no windows left in it. The siding was tattered wood and had whole sections of it that was missing. Honestly, I couldn't even see homeless people staying in it to keep warm at night.

The trees were thick here behind the house, but I could tell that in the front there was a street. I could hear the cars passing by occasionally, but it wasn't a busy street. I didn't know the city and had no idea where I was, so I really had no idea of where I should go from here. The elation of being free subsided as I realized that I was completely lost in a big city. There was something strange, though. There was something inside me, directing me, urging me to move.

I looked down at myself to assess my own injuries while I was mulling over my next move. I was dirty, but I didn't see any blood anywhere. I felt relatively okay. I was stiff and kind of sore, but that could have just been from running with the Warriors and combing the woods in the night. I didn't think I was really hurt, though. I wish I had a mirror to see what I actually looked like. I didn't want to go wandering about in public if my face was all dirty and my hair was matted-looking.

I had just escaped being kidnapped, and I was worried

about how I looked!

It wasn't really a kidnapping that I could explain, though, and if I looked okay I would have no need for explanations. I didn't need or want to draw attention to myself.

I decided that I needed to get to the street. It didn't matter how I looked, I had to get to Seline's. That was where she would be and probably Cabe also. If I were lucky I would meet up with the Warriors. I knew I couldn't take on Cabe by myself. I thought about the alternative of waiting on the Warriors' arrival, but I didn't think that was the best option. If I could get to Seline, maybe I could talk some sense into her. Maybe, after all, she could be saved, if not I could just kill her myself and be done with it.

If she were dead and Cabe couldn't have me, that would save the human world and put this battle on the fast track to being over with. In my mind, it was that simple. I knew I would never do the things that Avore expected me to do. I would never become evil and destroy this world. I would live in peace with William.

The street was close, and I found myself standing by a car looking in the window to see if I could get a better glimpse of myself. My hair didn't seem too shambled, and I ran my fingers through it quickly to get the few rats out. I didn't wear much makeup so my face was fine, and I couldn't see any particularly dirty spots. Actually it looked whiter than normal, and I was now noticing that my neck was beginning to ache.

I rubbed my hand across my cool flesh, and as I did I could feel the raised spots. I hastily looked closer into the window of the car, and I could see the bite marks. "Son of a bitch. He bit me." I felt the words slip from my lips and jumped back from the car. I had bite marks all over my neck. He had bitten me over and over again. I began to wonder how long I was down there and why my Warriors hadn't found me.

My mind was reeling as I began to walk down the street. I wasn't paying any attention to the people passing me until I noticed they were taking steps in the other direction to avoid me. The oddness that I felt inside of me was wrong on many different levels. I couldn't bear it. It was twisting and turning inside me and seemed to be guiding me in my navigation. I didn't want to go to

Seline's house like this, but I felt I had no choice. I felt like something was dragging me there against my will. I wanted to find the Warriors and be protected. My guts felt like they were being twisted out of me as the hunger struck me.

I looked around and could feel the tension building deeper inside with every person I saw. I could feel their pulse inside me and desperately wanted to attack them. I wanted to bite them. Nno, I wanted to eat them alive. I wanted to bathe in their blood and keep them inside me until I spewed with fulfillment.

I stopped and leaned against the wall that I had worked my way up to. I closed my eyes tightly and bent to put my hands on my knees. I wanted to hide my shame inside while I figured out what the hell was going on. Once I took a few breaths I could hear what was going on in their minds. "What a loon," followed by, "that bitch is crazy," and another, "should I call 911, no don't get involved." I had to get a better grip on myself. I made my way along the wall until I came to an opening between the buildings. I took it, and after what seemed like a long walk I was behind it where there was an alley to the left, a small parking lot to the right, and behind all of that were the woods. I opted to go straight into them.

I ran, letting the breeze and the tree limbs hit my face. I could feel welts forming on my bare skin from the force of the branches whipping against me. I hadn't realized I had run so long when there I was at the edge of the woods behind my sister's house. I could see it clearly from where I stood. I knew it was her house even though I had never been there. There was something drawing me towards it. It was pulling at my insides, and the pain was literally pushing me forward.

I wondered if the pain came from William. Maybe he was dead, and I hadn't realized it, or maybe he had died just as I had felt the first knife go deeper into my gut. If he were dead, I knew I could not survive without him. I could not live with this pain.

Then a more logical explanation took over, it was the fact that I had been bitten over and over again by Cabe. He had tainted anything that was left pure inside me. I could feel the coldness in my own pulse, which seemed to be beating sporadically.

I could feel death whispering in my ear. This death was not like Nuem when he had come to usher me home. This death was cold and calculated. This death would pursue me just to watch me fall and beg for my own breath. This was the death that would consume me and my soul. It would drag me into a darkness from which I would never escape.

I wanted to believe I had the answers lying inside me somewhere. I wanted to believe that after all this William would come up behind me and carry me off to someplace safe, warm, and comforting. I wanted to believe that, in spite of it all, Nuem would come and save me from the fate that I had somehow brought upon myself. However, the truth of the matter was, I was here alone at the edge of the woods, waiting for the invisible rope that had me tied to it to pull me down the hill and push me into my sister's house. The same house that I knew Seline and Cabe were in. The same house that I would finish dying in.

I wasn't certain how long I had been there, standing at the edge of the trees, until dusk began to settle over me. I could see the sun setting in the west, and I knew that I had to have been there for quite some time.

Kyhalu's voice echoed through the trees. Over and over it repeated what she had already told me.

"Remember, good or bad is neither just. Truth comes from the soul."

Her words were neither happy nor sad. They just were. I pulled myself together long enough to think of earlier, when I had been trapped in the candle. I was there and was stuck, and William had saved me. After that I was dead, and Nuem had brought me back. How is it now that I didn't have a savior to help me out?

Witches

How could I be destined to such a fate? I searched and could find no answer.

I looked down at Seline's house as I gathered the stamina to continue on. I felt as though I were dying as I marched down the hill towards the back of that house. I could certainly feel them both in there. I could see into Seline's mind, and Cabe was ravishing her. I felt the first pang of jealousy. I couldn't believe I had felt it, but I had. I not only wanted to kill her for the murder of our grandma, I wanted to kill her for her connection to Cabe. I really wanted to kill her. I didn't just want to kill her; I wanted to consume her, just as she had wanted to do to me. I was feeling the vengeance of a lifetime. With every step I wanted to destroy things, anything. The anger was taking me over. I was quickly becoming a monster.

As the changes took place in me I fought against them. I resisted them as best I could, but it was like holding your breath under water: finally a breath must be taken, even if it is the one that fills your lungs and ends your life. It is nature, and like drowning it was death. I could feel it sweep through me and take me over. However, instead of lying there on the grass, closing my eyes and finding whatever peace should have been waiting for me, I was stuck, still marching down this hill.

As I wiped my face with the back of my hand to remove the last of the sweat that my human body had secreted through its pores, I realized that my nails were longer, much longer. I had grown claws that should have belonged to a demon.

I recognized that the pale blue skin, which should have belonged to death, now covered my body. I wanted to weep but couldn't find the tears inside of me. My heart had quit beating and no longer pumped the blood through my veins, and I was quickly turning a bluish gray color. I could see it in my hands and arms, but mostly I could feel it inside. I could feel the pain of death pursuing me rapidly. I wanted to run from it, but couldn't. Each step pulled me one step closer to it. I could see the vision of it growing in my mind as I trudged on.

I was about half way there when I finally felt the intrusion of goodness into my despair. I could feel Samoda and Tarvoti before I saw them. I could feel their pulsating minds together as one. I could feel the vengeance that they had for everything evil. I could sense their instinctual hatred for me and had to turn from their faces as soon as they could see me.

"Kali, What the hell?" Samoda gasped at my sight.

Tarvoti had already gotten behind me and had a hold of me. I could feel her extended claws digging into my dying skin. The trickle of blood was smaller and thicker than it should have been. I could tell, and I could do nothing but smile. I could feel the wryness of the grin that was on my face. I could feel everything that was unholy surging through me. The only thing I could think of was how I would get away from these two and get to Seline so I could destroy her. Vengeance had taken hold in my soul and would destroy me from the inside out.

Samoda had taken on the role of trying to reason with me, while Tarvoti just physically restrained me.

"Kali, you know William is alive. He is going to be okay."

I knew she was trying to remind me of the goodness that had existed in my life. I didn't want to remember, though. I wanted to kill and devour.

"He will be here soon. He and Drake will be coming right over that hill at any moment. Come with us willingly. We don't want to hurt you."

Her voice had taken the tone that you might use with a child or someone who lacked understanding. I knew she was patronizing me, and it only fueled the anger that was raging in me. I couldn't restrain my tongue any longer as I began to scream at her.

"You filthy, self-absorbed whore! I hate you. Don't talk to me like a child. I'm much stronger than you give me credit for. You shouldn't underestimate my strength."

With that thought I had to laugh. It came out hysterically and manic. I couldn't believe I had said those things to her. I began to struggle with Tarvoti to free myself from her grip. Her sharp claws dug deeper into my arms. I knew she wanted to rip my head from my shoulders, and I turned my tongue on her.

"Why don't you do it, you scarred-up old bitch? You know you want to kill me. Go ahead and try. I will rip that calloused, dead heart right out of your chest and eat it in front of you."

I laughed again. I focused my confused mind on their dilemma. I knew they wanted to kill me. I wasn't quite sure why they hadn't just done it. Then I found it right there in Tarvoti's mind. Her duty was still to protect the human world, and she still thought that I was the key to doing that. I quit squirming under her power.

"Ah, I see. You can't kill me. I am the one who will save all of this. I am the one who will become the savior of man." I laughed harder at the prospect. "You know, Samoda, your 'visions' of me are total bullshit. I wouldn't save this world if my own life depended on it..." I paused to contemplate my next words. "... you see, it did. Look at me, I'm already dead. I have nothing left to complete. I have no life left to protect. Cabe has already unleashed the monster, this monster that I have become."

I felt my head fall towards the ground. I wanted to crawl into it for a moment. I wanted to take my place inside the tomb that should be mine, but a desire for vengeance once again spawned within my completely unbeating heart, and I was completely pissed off.

"Kali. You are wrong. You are just angry. You don't mean any of those things. I'm looking at you, and I still see goodness. I see you in pain. I see you in love with William. I see you, my friend."

I couldn't look Samoda in the eye right now. She would have broken me. She would have tipped the scales back to a place of some balance. I didn't want that, I wanted to go kill Seline.

I heard the thunder as I saw the flame flash across the sky. I couldn't concentrate on it enough to know what it was exactly. Tarvoti's mind was still so connected to mine that I saw it there though.

The flash in the sky was followed by a dragon swooping down and scooping us up. Tarvoti still had her claws stuck in me as we were thrown onto the beast by Samoda. Balcerak had come to Samoda in her time of need. He had given her an escape route in which she could take me safely away. As I spouted profanity, I was carried off into the darkness. I was carried off to a place where maybe my dead body could be healed. I was carried home, to my grandma's house that I had recently inherited, a place where all of this had started with a handsome stranger just a few days before.

CHAPTER SEVENTEEN

THE DEMON WITHIN

By the time Balcerak landed in the field that I called my backyard, my wrath had been quelled, but I was far from calm yet. I couldn't help the anger that had built inside me, and I couldn't help the things that had happened. I refused to take responsibly for it, despite the constant prodding from Tarvoti and Samoda. They had proclaimed that I was in control and could stop acting this way at any time. Even the beast that had carried us was trying to pry into my mind and plant a seed of serenity and some form of happiness. I could not see or hear it. I simply refused.

Cabe had not only taken goodness from me, he had replaced it with a deep hatred that I found justified. He placed a pain in me that ran deeper than my roots or my soul.

It wasn't until Tarvoti and Samoda dragged me into the house that I realized I could feel William. I wanted to tuck it away and not admit that I had been violated. I knew Cabe hadn't touched me sexually, but he had tainted me, and I knew William knew it. I then felt the first pang of guilt since I had awakened with the bite marks. I felt shame as I tried to ignore the presence of him in my mind. I wanted to hide from him, but couldn't.

Tarvoti dropped me onto the couch with a heavy thud. I listened to her as I tried to look through the boards that made up the floor.

"You would do well to stay put, because I'm to the end of my short rope with you and your antics. If I have to chase you down again, I may just *accidentally* kill you once and for all."

I knew she meant it, but I really didn't care. I almost wanted to jump up and run away just to have it all end. Every evil thing in the world had been piled upon me, and I was smothering under the weight of it. I hated it just like I hated everything else.

"Kali." The voice was smooth and strained. "My love. What has happened to you?"

I looked up to see William coming into the room. He was limping badly and looked pale. His eyes had become an amber shadow of what they had been. I tried to sink from his sight as he sat beside me.

"Kali, we are as one. I can feel your pain. I only hope you cannot feel mine."

His smile tried to light the room, but flickered out quickly. His hand reached for my shoulder, but I shunned it.

"I don't want your pity. I know I have become a monster."

I said it brazenly. I didn't want him to be bound to such a thing. I loved him still. The love that I had for him was buried deeper than anything in my soul and had not been destroyed by the demon, Cabe. I could feel it rising into my stomach and taking its place at the forefront of everything. It was the seed in which goodness could surely grow. I didn't know what I had become. I wasn't sure I wanted to know.

He pulled me to him and held me. His arms wrapped around me gently. I knew it was to shield his pain as well as mine. We stood, and I followed him slowly up to our room.

As I lay beside him, I realized the depth of our love. His thoughts were soothing. His eyes could see the pale blue that my skin had turned and found it beautiful. The green in my eyes had faded and only carried a slight hue of their original color. My hair was the only thing that remained its true color. I had turned into the black and white vision of death I had seen in my dream, but he would not allow my soul to become the same. He was there to save me.

The Warrior that lay inside William was weakened but not dead, and it showed in the razor sharp fangs that he revealed. He brought his own wrist to his mouth first and made a deep gash in it. He held it to my mouth for me to suckle from. I really wasn't surprised when he reached for my wrist and took it to his mouth. As we drank from one another I could feel the intense pleasure that it was bringing me, but I could also feel the strength that was growing inside of me.

The creature I had become was nothing short of lethal, and as the sweet liquid from William slid down my throat I could feel my own fangs emerge. They took their place under his skin as I drank. I knew instinctively that this process had been finished. I was now complete with who I had become. The monstrosity of my being was far from the perfection of that of the Warrior's, but it was deadly, it was different. I was completely new.

When I sat on the hill above Seline's house, I had prayed for this. I wanted to be saved like so many times before, and it had happened. William was here to heal me. He was here to heal my soul from the depraved evil that had infiltrated it.

As the sun came up, it felt hot on the exposed part of my back, which was facing the open window, hotter than it should have been. William could sense my discomfort. He got up and closed the old wooden shutters to shield my body from it. When he returned he lay behind me and wrapped his arms around me all the way. I rolled towards him in the cocoon he had made for me.

We lay there for hours just holding one another. We never slept, but at times I could feel the trance-like state that allowed me deep rest. I could feel the void that would be darkness in a normal world, where it would have meant sleep.

I never lost sight of the feeling of his goodness caressing me from the inside out. I wasn't yearning for him in a physical way. It was different now. I knew someday I would want him to make love to me again. I didn't know when that day would come, but for now, this was what I wanted and needed. I just needed his strength, and in a small way, he needed mine.

As the sun went down the silence was broken. I knew it was time to get up. I knew it was time to begin whatever future lay before me. It was time to learn this new body. The strength I felt was enormous, and I had to release some of it. I also knew the Quips were close again, too close.

I couldn't help but look in the mirror when I got up. It wasn't all that bad. I had seen myself through William's eyes, but I could see something slightly different than what he had seen. My skin was very pale but the veins that had riddled it earlier were gone. I could feel the lack of blood pumping. I didn't feel cold, but I knew I was. Even my emotions were chilled. I no longer felt the estrogen-fueled indecisiveness that accompanied the woman I was, just a couple of days ago.

William was soon behind me with his lips finding my neck. He kissed gently as he whispered to me.

"You are perfect. Together, we are perfect."

I couldn't help but smile at the changes I saw in him as well. His skin was a little paler, and his eyes shone with a new desire for vengeance. His unbeating heart was still set on the task at hand, but now he wanted Cabe and Seline as I did. He wanted them to suffer and fear him for a different reason. The urge for vengeance that I carried had flowed to him through my blood. He didn't want their demise for the good of the human world. He wanted them to writhe in pain for what they had done to me.

Samoda, Tarvoti, and Drake were in the living room when we went down the stairs. I could feel them there. I could feel everything, actually. I could even feel the smaller animals in the woods. I could feel their pulses burning in my throat as they ran as quickly as they could away from the Quips that were coming closer to the house. All of them stopped at the tree-line.

"I don't know if you can be saved completely, Kali." Samoda

said rather nonchalantly. Her eyes only grazed me slightly, but she knew I understood what she meant.

"I really don't give a shit what you think." I took a short moment to glance at all of them, "…or any of you for that matter."

"We are all friends here. Our duties may waiver, but our cause is the same. So, let's not draw a line between us. At least until this is over." Drake never looked at us as he spoke. He kept his focus on the window he was peering out of.

Tarvoti didn't have to speak. I knew she was desperately searching for a connection that had been broken. She was looking for the place where she and I had a common ground. She was trying to find the Strega link that we had endured since my birth. It must have been a link that was broken with my death, because since my rebirth was completed with William's blood, it had been broken. I knew she couldn't find my thoughts, yet I knew hers. Samoda was kind enough to let her know.

I couldn't help but enjoy my newfound power. I had always been so weak and had never known anything else. I had been enlightened to the supremacy of the other realms and now had my own strengths. I could feel the fear in the room. Everyone around me knew that I would not be easily removed. I had staked my claim to a new life, and I would stand my ground at any cost. I knew the only toll left to pay would be a permanent one. Nuem had warned me of that. There was nothing left to do but die a death, a true death, one that would last for eternity, and that was not a price I would be willing to pay. It was a toll that would have to be taken from me.

I smiled as I turned and walked out of the room. William was right behind me. As I stepped out into the night air, I felt a freedom that I had never felt. I wanted to run into the woods, but I restrained myself and began to compose a plan. I knew the Quips would do as I asked of them. In a strange turn of events, I was their queen. I would turn them on their maker. I would send them back with a message. I would send them back to Cabe, not to destroy him, but to bring him and Seline to me. Oh yes, that was my plan. It would be my blood that would destroy them. It would be my death that brings truth. In a way that I could have never foreseen, the Danbue, Kyhalu, was completely right, and I understood what she had told me. I heard the little giggle from the trees that I knew was hers.

I had stopped walking in the field back behind the house, and I raised my hands to the sky to gather more power into me. I felt my face twist into something that didn't resemble anything human. I could actually feel my body writhe with an ecstasy unknown, as I felt the change take place. I didn't have to face William to see what he was seeing. I could see my body lengthen. I could see the claws that were longer than the Warrior's taking their shape at the ends of my elongated fingers. I could have manipulated the moon had I chose to.

I didn't have to see my face to know what it looked like. Its pale smoothness had been replaced and every vein that had been present as a human took its place. They raised themselves into a map of destruction. They pulsated as though they were pumping cold syrup through them. I knew my eyes had become a glowing white color, and I could see everything as if I was wearing night vision glasses. They weren't seeking out the heat as normal night vision glasses would have been, instead they found every cold, calculated presence that was around me. I could see every Quip squirming in the woods, and I knew they were waiting for my command.

The voice that was building inside me was instinctual. I didn't have to search for the words or reach for a book to tell me what to say. It was just there. I knew what I wanted to tell them, but it wouldn't come out in the form of a language anyone could understand except the Quips. They would know what I was saying. They would understand my demands, and they would follow them to the letter.

I took a deep intentional breath into my lungs to make them work properly, and as I breathed out, the scream of the words felt as though they would burst the air that carried them. Everything around them was blown like a hurricane force wind being funneled through a small channel.

"You wretched demons, the wrath of defiance is death. The final death that will take you straight to the hell that you fear. I am your queen and more powerful than your creator. You must bring him to me. You must have him hunt me and ensnare him in my trap. Only then will you find freedom. Only then will you find a death that does not sentence you to damnation. Now go and have him meet me north of here in a place that is familiar. You will know where I am, I will summon you when I get there. Go. I command you as your Queen."

As the screeching winds came to a halt, I knew there were three among the dozens that had chosen to defy me. I never felt my feet find the ground as I darted into the woods after them. I was faster than I had ever imagined, and I found them quickly and easily. I satiated the arid thirst that had burnt through me. I would not tolerate their disobedience. I sank my fangs into the same creatures that had tormented me so badly. The same creatures that had nearly taken my human life as they burned me with their acidic insides were now slaking my thirst as I took their souls into a world of eternal torture and damnation, and I enjoyed it.

As I calmly walked out of the woods the Warriors were standing there. The thoughts that were going through their minds were muddled with a slight fear. Tarvoti couldn't believe what she was seeing. She knew I was strong now, she had sensed that. She also knew that I wasn't like them, I had a different heart and a thirst for vengeance. Drake was slightly amused, and just like a man, was weighing the outcome of a battle between us. Samoda was a little taken back at my actual strength. She was also a little disturbed that she hadn't opted to destroy me when it would have been easier. She wondered if this was what was meant to be. If I would truly be the means to fulfill their duty, or if something had gone treacherously wrong in the plan. William stood with them, but in no way felt like them. He loved me. He was true to me and my cause. He had lost the devotion he had begun with, had replaced it with a devotion to me. I knew there was nothing I would do that could make him turn from me, and he was by my side in an instant. I was now the one in control, and they all knew that in some small way, they should fear me.

CHAPTER EIGHTEEN

CHASING DEATH

I knew the best way for all of us to travel together was in the SUV, but it didn't make the ride any easier. I didn't like being confined in such a small space with the Warriors. I didn't like Tarvoti on one side of me and Samoda on the other. William and Drake were up front and Drake was driving. He knew where to go as we traveled up the rural highway. I had already told them where the meeting would take place.

It actually seemed like a lifetime since I had traveled this road when I had gotten the news of Grandma's death. I had dreaded the trip that day to the family farm almost as much as I dreaded this trip back to my own home. The town was much bigger than the one-horse town I had grown up in, but still would not be considered a city by any means.

I could see the dread in Samoda's thoughts as we passed over the bridge to the springs that marked us as being close. I thought of the irony that she had actually lived in the same place. I was also surprised that I hadn't known her. I guess even in a small town it's not realistic that you know absolutely everyone. It was apparent that we had run in much different circles. At any rate, her apprehension was based around seeing her human family. She didn't want to bring a battle to their home, and that was exactly what she thought I was doing. She had hoped that maybe they had moved away and, if not, had steeled her resolve to protect them. She knew I was aware of all of this, and it was as though she were sending me a warning.

When we got into town, Drake had slowed to observe the speed limit and not draw attention to us. I was glad the ride had only been a couple of hours, and I could tell by the internal clock ticking away inside of me that daybreak would be coming very soon. I had enough of the demon's blood inside of me that, even though it wouldn't kill me, it would be very uncomfortable to endure the direct sunlight hitting my skin.

We drove slowly through the newer part of town and made a right on Main Street. I felt a slight pang of compassion when I looked up at the building that towered across the street where we turned. I knew it to be the local newspaper, and I could see the light burning brightly in the corner office on the second floor. I knew it was the reporter that had done a story on "The Hippie Shop" a while back. He was a hard worker, and I only hoped that he would finish his work today and go home for the night tonight.

I knew this battle would begin and end in this small town with the coming of darkness. I wished that I could have found a place in my heart to take it somewhere else, but I could not. This was the spot that would end it. This was the town that would see the end of this battle tonight.

As we drove past the newer shops that were well maintained on Main Street you could actually see the difference in the storefronts the closer we got to my shop. When we got in front of the old block building that still had the faded paint on the side reading "Storage," we were there. In the front over the door was my shingle. It hung straight out and wasn't fancy or decorated. It simply said "The Hippie Shop." Drake pulled the car over, and we all got out. I went around back to go in the back door. I had never had a key for the front.

I reached down to get the key from under the sill that I had hid there when I rented the place many years before. After jiggling it in the lock the door opened, and I was in a comfortable spot. The rear of the shop had offered me many nights crafting things to sell. It had doubled as an apartment for me as well. I smiled as I looked around. I had always been fond of the old treadle sewing machine and had sewn many garments on it.

I made my way through the beaded doorway into the front part of the store and opened the door for the others to come in. William was the first in, followed by Tarvoti. I locked it back behind them. I didn't want any customers to wander in though the day in search of the perfect little thing while we were resting.

Drake and Samoda had already left to go check on her family. The last she had known they actually lived a few blocks from here, and she was worried about them. As close as they were, I felt her relief when she learned that they no longer lived there. Samoda could now focus on the task at hand, and they were back to the shop quickly.

I stretched out on the bed with William as they all found a spot to lie down. We would need our rest tonight, and that's what we did, we rested.

When the sun was heading to the west I found myself coherent and free from the trance of broad daylight.

"You know you are over-estimating your power, don't you? You are strong, Kali, but not near as much as you think." Samoda's voice was soft and confident. I knew she believed what she was saying.

"I know you believe that. I also know that you do not understand my need for vengeance, and I don't blame you. Seline has destroyed every single thing that I have held dear..." I paused to allow that to sink in, "...and I will kill her. I will kill her, and I will kill Cabe. It is my vengeance that will save your humans. It will save Nuem's humans.

"This was not my choice, it was my destiny. I had little choice, if any at all, in these events. It must have been written before time. You know this though, Samoda.

"I will do it my way. I will do it with William by my side, and when this battle is done, you Warriors will leave William and I to ourselves. You will no longer badger us to be a part of you. He is different from you now. He and I are a new species, a new breed, without your compassion for the duty that you hold so dear. We will pursue our own fate, together."

"I understand more than you think I do. You will need our assistance."

Those were the last words spoken before everyone else rose from their own darkness. The sun was barely a sliver on the horizon when I knew they were coming. I felt the thunder of their steps with each one. I could tell they were getting closer as the monster inside me began to rumble with her own fury.

Tarvoti pulled a book from the bag that she toted with her and tossed it in my direction. It was the old leather bound book that I had opened with my own blood.

"You have ignored this far too long. Before we move any further, you must read."

I reluctantly opened the book and began to read on the first page.

May the evil of a thousand lives keepeth away from my soul. May I draw strength from the spirits that guide me and keep the demons of the past and future in their place. Do not let me draw breath of air that has been tainted by demons.

The words ran through my mind and into my body as though they were becoming part of me. It seemed like it was a little too late for this, and I wanted to jump and run away from them. I felt as though I were being held to the page as I read on.

Spirit of fire, burn the evil from this place. Spirit of wind blow him down before he can enter. Spirit of water, drown him out to keep her safe. Spirit of earth, bury him deep within. In Nuem's name I ask this. I ask that death escort me to the world beyond this one before evil taketh my soul.

I could feel the twisting wrath inside me again. I closed my eyes to shut out the inevitable, and I knew that this death was not the death I had hoped for. It was not ideal, but it was the one that I had been given. I would deal with it once this battle was over.

For now, the hunger in the pit of my stomach was calling me. It was twisting my mind into the monster inside me. The sweet smell of the sage and lavender was no longer my solace. It reminded me of what I would never be again, and I held a disdainful contempt for what it used to represent. I wanted to smother it.

As I shoved the book shut with a thud, I realized I must feed. I was, after all, much more than I had ever been. I had been touched by Nuem and dragged through a world of demons. I had been privileged to befriending the Danbue. I had seen angels in this world and the next. I had been mated with the mightiest of the worlds, in the form of a Warrior named William, and I had been stolen away and kidnapped by dragons and devils. Maybe I was a little self-serving at this point, and I really didn't care if I was, I deserved it.

As I looked up half-crazed and filled with the desire of death, I prepared to walk out of the store and feed on the demons that were quickly closing in. I was ready to walk into my destiny as a murdering monster. I ignored the whisper that echoed behind me saying, *don't give in, I have not forsaken you.* The only thing my mind could wrap around was the thirst that was tearing my guts apart and the words, *Segreti delle Streghe solo il sangue definirà il libro: "Secrets of the Strega. Only the blood will define the book."*

Tarvoti stood between me and the door. She moved to allow me through as the door opened itself to obey my command. I practically floated across the concrete sidewalk behind the store.

When I came close to the grassy area where a few trees grew, they hid in waves from me. I could see the green blades turn black and fall to the ground before me.

I didn't have to sniff the air. I could smell Cabe and Seline to the south. That would be perfect, maybe we could spare the town the brunt of the destruction if we were to head them off. To the south there were lots of wooded areas where the battle could take place. I took off, and the Warriors were right behind me.

We ran through what was left of town and headed southwest into the woods. We didn't run far, and I stopped in the middle of the rural highway. I could not see the Warriors but I knew they were close by in the woods. I could feel each of them. William was edgy and not liking leaving me out there on my own. He knew my strength though, and held his reserve.

It was only a second before I was face to face with my twin. Her body pulsated much like mine. She had gone through some changes herself. I was certain that the dress she wore had at some point had been white and probably flowed around her body like a cloud. Now it was torn here and there and splattered with blood. It was dingy looking from the dirt and water that she had just run through.

My feet were firmly planted on the asphalt in a defensive stance as she circled around me slowly. The monster inside me had completely emerged during the run.

"Well, well, well, Kali. I see you have done well since I last saw you. I must admit that I'm surprised to see you alive. I figured your *friends* would have eaten you alive."

I didn't respond. I just watched her. She was trying to taunt me, and I wasn't going to let it work. I would not lose sight of the reason I was here, and that was simply to kill her and Cabe.

"Where's your demon, Seline?" I asked earnestly. Her laughter filled the air.

"Oh, he said I could have you to do with as I pleased. He has given me powers that you won't believe."

As she finished the sentence she hit me hard, sending me flying up the road. I landed gracefully on my feet and ran for her. We met in mid-air. My foot caught her right up beside her head. The blow sent her through the air, and I landed in a crouch. She disappeared into the woods.

"Come out, come out, wherever you are, dear sister." I hollered the words as I looked in every direction. The new sense of vision I possessed made it easy to spot her. I ran into the woods after her. When I caught her I grabbed her by the throat and threw her violently to the ground. I felt the blow as she landed and knew that this would not be an easy task. Killing her could also kill me, and I could not do that until Cabe showed up. He had to go first. I let loose an inhuman scream that had built up in my chest to signal the Quips to bring him to me.

I saw the confusion in Seline as I did it. I had found something that she had not. She had no idea of their language and could not understand what I had done.

Seline was still stunned, lying where I had thrown her. Before she could recover or I could reach her, she was surrounded by the Warriors who emerged from the woods, drawn by my cry and the sounds of our battle. I saw that our group had now been reinforced by a couple of other Warriors, members of one of the nearby clans who Samoda had summoned to battle.

The Warriors had already grabbed her and had her in tow when I got to them. They were taking her deeper into the woods. Until a few days ago I had not known that there was a clan not far from here. They had settled here after the battle last year and were living in an old house outside of town. The townspeople had accepted them as transplants from the city. When we walked in I recognized a couple of them that had wandered into my shop before. They quickly helped to secure Seline in the basement with chains to ensure that she wouldn't escape.

The rest of us returned to the woods in search of Cabe. We could smell him and knew he was close. Cabe was there. He was trying to escape, but a mass of golden-skinned Quip had poured from the woods and surrounded him. The Quip, obedient to me, their queen, had blocked his retreat. Individually they were no match for Cabe's strength, and in a moment he could have fought his way free, but he did not have a moment. William had arrived, and I was right behind him. I could feel William pulsating with an unrivaled anger. I knew when he laid his first claw on Cabe. I could feel it. I could almost taste it as he sank his teeth into him. Before I could get there he had extinguished him completely. There was nothing left but a shell of a demon that had terrorized me since I had met him. I looked down at William with the demon still splattered on his face. His rage had lessened after he tore him apart, and I knew it was all but over.

When we got back to the old house where Seline was being held prisoner, I headed straight for the basement. I smacked her hard across the face. The power I wielded stung my own face, but I didn't care. I would rip her limb from limb.

"I hope you're happy to have destroyed everything, Seline. You have always been a whiney spoiled brat. There was never an excuse—"

She cut me off, spitting words at me. "I have always lived in your shadow. It's only fitting that I die in it also, you self-righteous bitch. You are no better than I am."

I couldn't help but laugh in her face, and as I stood there looking at her it all came together in my mind. I had become very much like her. I had allowed myself to say some of the same things to the beings that had loved me and tried to help me. I had felt the same vengeance and feelings. I had been self-righteous and cold. I had become everything that I had despised.

I raised my eyes towards the sky. It was shielded from me by the ceiling, but I looked past it into the world that I knew existed above us all. I turned my thoughts to Nuem, the God that I knew was there, and I prayed. I asked for forgiveness. I asked for guidance. I asked for peace. I asked that he break the bond that I had with this demon. I wanted to be free, even if that meant death. I was ready for this death to be over. I was ready for the world to end for me. I completely ignored the pleas that came from Seline as I kept my mind focused on Nuem as I begged him to come and end it for me. Whatever the toll, I was ready to pay it.

I felt the panic in William's soul as Tarvoti came through the door and began to descend the stairs. I could see Drake and Samoda holding him back with all of their might. I could see him struggling to free himself from their bonds. He would have ripped her apart if he could have reached her. He knew what she was doing. She was the one that was finally ending this battle.

I knew her every thought with each step she took. She didn't want to do this, but she had no choice. Nuem wasn't allowed here, and she was doing his bidding. He had asked her to do this. He had heard my pleas and was answering them. I knew that she was doing what was right in the eyes of all that was good. That didn't include me anymore.

She walked past me without even looking at me. She raised the sword that she was carrying high above her head. I couldn't help but see the jewel-encrusted handle. I knew it was the sword of my vision. It was the one that I had already held. It was the same one that Seline herself had held.

I would not fight her. I would not resist the death that I knew was coming. I silently said my apologies to Nuem and asked him to care for my Warrior. I asked him to ease his pain and make him whole again. I wanted nothing more than to leave him in peace. I could tell by the screams that came from William that he was in pain, and his mourning would be dreadful, but I also knew that he was strong. He would heal.

As the sword came down, I felt it. My body fell to the floor even as Seline's fell limp in the chains that bound her. I could see the vision of everything fading to blackness as William ran for me. He too faded from me as he held my limp body. Then there was nothing left, nothing but the darkness that consumed me.

CHAPTER NINETEEN

A WARRIOR'S GRIEF

As a full-fledged Elder, I felt the grief that was plaguing William. It pained me deeply to see him hurting, but I knew it was for the best for all of us. I was saddened to see him holding onto the corpse of Kali. It broke my unbeating heart to see him carry her into the woods, but I knew where he was going. He was returning her to her home to be buried next to her family. He needed to give her a proper burial, one that she would have wanted.

He had regained the obligation of duty to Nuem, but a piece of him was gone, and he would never return to the same Warrior that he had been before this. Kali had changed him for all of eternity, and the pain that dwelt in his soul was everlasting.

With the money that we had access to it would be easy to cover up everything. He already had it planned in his mind, and it would play out just as he devised.

The next morning he went Mr. Button's office and made certain that he could show the correct legal documents for everything. He was now the only legal relative of Kali Rose Marriot Eaton and was the heir to her family farm as well as in charge of her funeral.

Drake, Tarvoti, and I went to pay our last respects. No matter what we said to him, he was still in mourning and paid us no attention. He needed more time and more healing. Among us only Tarvoti knew his pain directly.

The monument that he had built in her memory was more than out of place in the Mount Pilot cemetery. It was huge, with angels to watch over where she lay. The rose bush that he planted there had overtaken her burial site overnight. The roses that bloomed were bright crimson. Each petal had a small X towards the end that was as black as night. The thorny bushes that they bloomed from were thick and lethal. As each petal fell they landed in a protected thicket, to lay there and wither in peace, just as Kali had done. She had gone in peace while praying for peace.

Drake and I decided to stay on, in my hometown, with the clan that had taken stake to this area. The big house that they lived in had plenty of room, and they welcomed us openly. It had been long enough since my death, 10 years, and I found a comfort in being home. It would be nice to be able to watch the area and see people from my past. Tarvoti went back to the Elder's Den in the heart of the Carpathian Mountains. She was much more comfortable there and could visit Arxies any time she chose.

We also knew we needed to stay close to William, and we visited often. It was a short run for us. Each time we visited he had done more to the farm that he had inherited. He had it looking more like a mansion than the old farm house that it had been. Drake and I were certain that he was fixing it up to match the visions that he had seen in Kali's mind. It was part of the healing process for him. He had mated with a human and now had some human urges. We were patient and tried to understand the grief he was going through.

Summer and fall came and went without any major events at all. Things were rather mundane in our life, and that was okay. We were all actually enjoying the visionless, commonplace life that we had settled into. The Clan that we had taken residence in was strong, and we all enjoyed each other's company very much.

Drake and I did more human things than I had done since

Witches

I had died 11 years earlier. We went to movies and vacationed. I found where my human family had moved to and checked in on them every so often.

Today, being the last day of the year, December 31, 2022, we decided to go see William. Drake and I took our normal run through the trees, jumping over the creeks and enjoying the crisp winter air.

When we got there we knew something was amiss. The last time we had visited, William had looked good. He had been talkative and anxious to show us the work he had done on the farm. This time, he looked weary when he came out to meet us. The thing most out of place was the void in his mind. I couldn't get through it. Something was holding him hostage from me, and the Warrior inside me could feel it and began to twist her way out of me.

"Hello friends." He said it with a half-hearted smile as he wrapped a single arm around Drake. He didn't look at me.

"What's going on William?" I said with angst in my voice. I tried to catch his eyes but he turned them towards the ground.

"Nothing Samoda. I've just been…" He paused, thinking of what to say next. I couldn't see what his dilemma was, but I could see that he certainly had one. "I need to show you all something."

He ran for the woods, and we were right behind him. We followed him until we stopped at the edge of the woods around Mount Pilot Cemetery.

The light snow that had fallen the day before created a blanket of white that didn't quite cover the ground. The black ground peeked out here and there.

My eyes followed Drake's and William's until they found the only colorful thing in the area. There mixed with the dormant foliage were the colors of green and red entwined together over the grave where Kali had been put in her resting place, the place that was supposed to be her "final" resting place.

Something was obviously stirring in the ground, under the bright crimson flowers and lush carpet of green leaves that mixed with the lethal thorns that looked as sharp as razors waiting for their next victim. The stench that caught in my throat was overwhelming. I could feel my fangs growing in search of it. I lost control of the Warrior inside as I leaped towards the grave site.

"I kept them trimmed back for a while." William looked down as he continued. "Then, I couldn't. I can't get close enough to them. They…" I could see the shame in his mind. "…they won't let me trim them anymore."

I reached towards the razor-sharp thicket and then saw what he meant. Each thorn stood at attention. They had armed themselves with a toxic sap that would be injected into any victim that found themselves close enough. I could actually see the thorns pulsing with anticipation.

"Samoda, don't touch it." Drake's voice was strong as he warned me. "Do not touch it, my love." His hand was around my arm before his words were even finished, pulling me back.

I had the urge to ignore him and plunge forward into the thorns. I wanted to tear them out from their roots. I wanted to dig at the ground until I found her. Then I wanted to consume every ounce of her soul until she disappeared from existence. I wanted to rid this world of her once and for all, but I couldn't.

I felt Woden drop Tarvoti close by. As she ran through the woods towards us, I knew that she had been given direction. The thoughts that pushed her forward were consumed with regret. She knew that she should have consumed her, as she had Seline. She knew that her undead body had been immune to the mere human death that she had invoked on her. She knew that evil had taken her from the inside out now, and she was no longer the Kali that we had known.

In her mind, it had all come together. Kali had been protected by her grandmother and even herself, then she had been protected by William, and now, in death, she was being protected by these thorns that covered her.

Tarvoti knew that she was literally being fed by the blood that they collected. The blood of the humans that had come to look at the beautiful growth had been plentiful. The anomaly of the undying bush had already received much attention and people had been coming to look. The occasional sightseer would try to pluck a rose from it, and it would have found its prey. It gathered food for Kali, the one that lay underneath. It had even fed from William.

She knew that it was growing and creating something different. It was creating a Warrior. Everything that she had endured during her human life and everything that had ensued afterwards was boiling together. It was smelting a creature that we would have to deal with. She also knew we had to wait. There was no turning the clock forward. We would have to wait for the beast to be created, so we could end its miserable existence.

For now, we had to deal with William, who had been infected with the thorn's venom. He looked worse by the moment. His eyes had taken a wild abandon. The black pupils mixed with a blue that could be found in a night sky, but their whites had red pulsing through them. It gave William a look of death. It gave him a look that resembled the rawness that pulsated from the bush that covered the grave.

As I looked into his eyes, I knew he wasn't certain how much more he could take. He had gone from one of the strongest Warriors in existence to one of the weakest. He had survived mating with this human who had taken his unbeating heart. He had also survived her death. He had been torn in two, and yet he survived.

I also knew that he wasn't a traitor. He was pure in his duty. He just didn't know what to do anymore. He wanted to do the just thing, and that was the seed that we would grow.

With Drake in the lead we headed back to the farm where this had started. As I ran, I asked Nuem to have mercy on my friend and brother Warrior. I asked that he take the pain from him and heal him from the inside out and as we ran, William was swept up by Woden.

I knew that he was being taken from us. I knew that he had no place here right now. We could not heal him or even salve his wounds, they were much too deep. Only Nuem could find the words. Only Nuem would have the medicine that could soothe his soul. Only Nuem had the cure for what plagued him.

I felt Tarvoti breathe a sigh of relief as our God's wings wrapped around him and he found comfort. She likened it to her own experience when she had lost her love. She knew William had been hurt worse than she had, and she found compassion in the pit of her soul for him.

William had transformed the old farmhouse into somewhat of a mansion. It was the perfect place for us to stay. William had inadvertently made us a home here. He had reinforced everything to withstand our size and suit our tendencies. The carvings that he had been driven to etch into the wooden trims were done so with his own claws on nights that he sought peace and guidance from our God. The ornate designs were masterpieces that replicated the ones in the stairs at the castle on Atheria. This place was now our home here on earth. It had started as a shrine to a lost love and had become a haven for us. The irony of the whole situation seemed nearly funny to me. I smiled as I settled in.

I walked into the only room that had not been completely renovated. I thought of the future and the war that was constantly looming on the horizon. I thought of the battle that would come, and I knew it would be a while. I hadn't had any visions of it yet, but I was certain they would come. I knew that the whole ordeal would come about in its own time. I looked at the room through a different set of eyes and realized that all of the things in here were simple, so much more so than the eternity that I had been gifted. Everything in this room was nothing more than the remnants of life.

About the Author

Georgia L. Jones was born in Columbia, Missouri on September 21st, 1968. In 1992 she settled in the beautiful Ozarks town of Lebanon, Missouri, where she has lived since.

At a young age Georgia learned the value of getting lost in a good book. She has always enjoyed reading and letting her imagination run wild. In her early teenage years she began to put her own stories down on paper as she plunked out the words

Over the years Georgia has harbored the dream of being a published author and written many short stories. On January 10, 2010 she embarked on the dream as she began to bring the characters from her first novel, "Legends of Darkness", to life. Upon completion in June 2010 she realized that it was not a single book but a series and created the concept of the series "Remnants of Life".

On September 5, 2010 the "Remnants of Life" series was contracted through a small press publishing house out of Louisville, KY., and so her career began. Through that press, Blackwyrm Publishing, Georgia L. Jones published the first two books in the series, Legends of Darkness and Witches, took part in several anthology works both as an author and editor, and created a new character to add to her own multi-faceted personality, Smarty Mic Smartypants who endeavors into the more cynical and snarky side of life. In September of 2015 she became part of the Seventh Star Press Family which is based out of Lexington, KY. The second edition of the first two books in the "Remnants of Life" series as well as the third book in the series are currently contracted through them.

When her muse isn't dragging her to lands unknown, you will find her hanging out with her family and friends in the Novalunium Paranormal Mansion, the 1840 farmhouse that she calls home as well as home base for the small Paranormal Research Group that her and a couple of friends have founded.

Also Available from Seventh Star Press,
the horror stylings of
Michael West!

Trade Paperback ISBN: 9780983740209
eBook ISBN: 9780983740216

Trade Paperback ISBN: 9781937929718
eBook ISBN: 9781937929725

Trade Paperback ISBN: 9781937929954
eBook ISBN:9781937929831

Trade Paperback ISBN: 978-1-937929-18-3
eBook ISBN: 978-1-937929-19-0

Now available!   A Seventh Star Press Anthology
from editor Michael West!

eBook ISBN: 978-1-937929-69-5
Softcover ISBN: 978-1-937929-60-2

Vampires Don't Sparkle! poses the question: What would
you do if you had unlimited power and eternal life?

Would you...go back to high school? Attend the same classes
year after year, going through the pomp and circumstance
of one graduation after another, until you found the perfect
date to take to prom? Would you...spend your days moping
and brooding, finding your only joy in a game of baseball
on a stormy day? Or would you...do something else?

The authors of this collection have a few ideas; some fanciful,
some humorous, and some as dark as an endless night.

Join us, and discover what it truly means to be "vampyre."

From Bram Stoker Award-winning Editor Michael Knost!

Softcover ISBN:
978-1-937929-61-9
eBook ISBN:
978-1-937929-62-6

Writers Workshop of Science Fiction and Fantasy is a collection of essays and interviews by and with many of the movers-and-shakers in the industry. Each contributor covers the specific element of craft he or she excels in. Expect to find varying perspectives and viewpoints, which is why you many find differing opinions on any particular subject.

This is, after all, a collection of advice from professional storytellers. And no two writers have made it to the stage via the same journey-each has made his or her own path to success. And that's one of the strengths of this book. The reader is afforded the luxury of discovering various approaches and then is allowed to choose what works best for him or her.

Featuring essays and interviews with:

Neil Gaiman, Orson Scott Card, Ursula K. Le Guin, Alan Dean Foster, James Gunn, Tim Powers, Harry Turtledove, Larry Niven, Joe Haldeman, Kevin J. Anderson, Elizabeth Bear, Jay Lake, Nancy Kress, George Zebrowski, Pamela Sargent, Mike Resnick, Ellen Datlow, James Patrick Kelly, Jo Fletcher, Stanley Schmidt, Gordon Van Gelder, Lou Anders, Peter Crowther, Ann VanderMeer, Joh Joseph Adams, Nick Mamatas, Lucy A. Snyder, Alethea Kontis, Nisi Shawl, Jude-Marie Green, Nayad A. Monroe, G. Cameron Fuller, Jackie Gamber, Amanda DeBord, Max Miller, Jason Sizemore.

Apocalyptic and Dystopian Modern Fantasy From Stephen Zimmer!

Book One: The Exodus Gate
Softcover ISBN: 9780615267470
eBook ISBN: 9780982565674

Book Two: The Storm Guardians
Softcover ISBN: 9780982565636
eBook ISBN: 9780982565681

Book Three: The Seventh Throne
Softcover ISBN: 9780983740247
eBook ISBN: 9780983740223

From H. David Blalock, The Angelkiller Triad!
A trilogy that fuses the digital realms with those of the
supernatural, in a world where in the beginning... evil gained
the upper hand.

The Angelkiller Triad

Featuring cover art and interior illustrations by
the award-winning Matthew Perry

Softcover ISBN: 9781937929732
eBook ISBN: 9781937929749

Softcover ISBN: 9780983740230
eBook ISBN: 9780983740285

Softcover: 978-1-937929-55-8
eBook: 978-1-937929-57-2

Urban Fantasy from John F. Allen!
Meet Ivory Blaque!

Softcover: 978-1-937929-16-9
eBook: 978-1-937929-17-6

In The God Killers, the first book of The God Killers Legacy, former professional art thief Ivory Blaque is hired to procure a pair of antique pistols and gets much more than she bargained for when several attempts are made on her life.

Her client turns out to be a shadowy government agent who reveals that she is descended from a race of immortals, and that the pistols are linked to her unique heritage and the special psychic gifts she possesses. He uses the memory of her father to guilt her into working for him.

Ivory eventually gives in to his request, and in return, he presents her with her father's journal, which was written in an unbreakable code. Bishop believes that she is the only one capable of breaking the code and unlocking the plans of the vampire hierarchy. But when the city's top vampire is a sexy incubus with an attraction for her and she's assigned a hot new lycan enforcer to protect her, she finds herself caught between two sets of rock hard abs.

To regain her autonomy, clear her name, unlock the secrets of her past, and protect the lives of those closest to her, Ivory must play along with the forces trying to manipulate her. Ivory's life is rapidly spiraling out of control and headed for an explosive conclusion which she just might not survive.

www.ingramcontent.com/pod-product-compliance
Lightning Source LLC
Chambersburg PA
CBHW050426260626
47156CB00003B/1168